Street S

To Mohran

Thank You

Clayton Crawford

By

Clayton Crawford

Dedications

To my Mother and Sisters

About the Author

I like Star Trek, Star Wars, X-Files, and Comic Books -- Go Spidey Go! I like to read and I write on Medium... I am Canadian, eh!

Table of Contents

Zerth Jungle

Camouflage images moved blending into the forest.

The talking forest, birds, alien ones and other creatures produced a continuous foreign language.

A steady simulating cool air blew through the jungle of Zerth, totally opposite of what would be expected. One would imagine lung squeezing, choking humidity, being suffocated by a pillow case. Zerth defied many accepted rules.

Dreadlock Trees created a canopy filtering the sunshine. The Dreadlocks were sprinkled all over the landscape, the main stick in these neck of the woods, and they had natural predators such as the Fangclever rodents which would peck on the thick bark chipping away for food. And the Fangclever rodents had enemies, Toothy Jaw-Trees that could stretch their a branches and snatch one or two perhaps three Fangclever rodents, and opening their mouths stuffing a Fangclever inside its mouth. Blood and drool would squeeze out of the Jaw-Tree mouth as the teeth would chew and chew and chew crushing the bones of a Fangclever.

Seven recent graduate Street Surgeons from the Pangaea Hammurabi University followed two mentors, one Squadron Leader and the other person designated as the Team Leader, through the woods for a total of nine. Each student wore an identical battle suit and around their waist a utility belt. The arm sleeves had a distinct medical emblem the Caudexes, but the Squadron Leader and Team Leader patches displayed blue body sphinxes with a winged coiled creature coiled around. The creature was officially known on Moonsteep as a Serum and extremely poisonous. And, any intelligent care giver would realize their education originated from Moonsteep Medical Empire. The students and mentors would be equal footing with the mythical medical god, also mysteriously named Serum. He was the one god long ago saved the entire population of Moonsteep people with a Mahagick potion.

Kidney T. (Thyroid) Fungus walked next to Sheranda Q'arlette Hammurabi, an activity he enjoyed. At thirty they were considered Moonagers, the classification of age from twenty-one to seventy-one and adulthood next classification was Moonknhurd, and their Mentors were Moonknuhurds. Everyone in the Street Surgeon Troop originated from the planet Pangaea, but often the nicknamed was used, Moonsteep.

Kidney, a monster/ swamp person, towering eight feet five inches, three hundred and forty-two pounds. He was athletic according to Street Surgeon standards. He a Cyclops green eye and for protection he wore a special goggle lens over it. The all-purpose battle one-piece suit had multiple flap pockets for additional medical equipment and the Mahagick Engineers referred to the fabric as Smart-tech keeping the users safe, cool and warm according to the weather conditions. The Smart-tech helped keep them camouflaged, blending into the forest. "*Zerth's jungle is not much different than where I grew up on Moonsteep, my Bloodline is a member of the Swamp Nation of Indigenous People*," he thought.

Sheranda Q'arlette Hammurabi was recognized immediately as a Dewskinner, an indigenous person of the Twelve Multiverse Tribe or Befour Nation. The wings kind of gave away the secret, if she ever consider hiding her wings, and so that concept could not ever creep into her imagination. Her natural blue/white skin also was a distinguishing detail of her indigenous race that arrived on Pangaea seven millennia ago, but now the Multiverse Tribe were as much part of the Pangaeain world as the other races. "*Myself and my Bloodline and my people are the children of the long ago Tribe that arrived from somewhere, perhaps the Enochverse, planet Merth, places written into the Great Spirit Book and our people escaped an invasion army called, Synopaths, beings with TVs for heads and a screen for a face. Weird stuff for bedtime stories*," she thought.

Turning his head right to be sure his assigned teammate was not lagging, Kidney could not help notice Sheranda's lips. The curve of her upper lip somehow gave a distinct attractiveness.

"Why are you looking at me like that?" she accused in a suspicious manner.

"You are delirious, what you taking about," he rebutted

immediately defending himself and hiding his feelings.

“Why are you pausing?” Sheranda asked and allowed her wings to spread wide open and levitate her three meters. This was a good stretch, not necessarily showing off, she just needed to stretch.

“Sheranda,” Squadron Leader punched out a tone. A Dewskinner herself, she ascended greeting the recent grad. “Don’t show off. There are creatures in the Zerth forest that may wish to attack you, taste you such as a Jaw-Tree,” she continued.

“Sssssorrry, Squadron Leader, Kayla,” Sheranda replied purposely stretching the letter ‘S’ and ‘R’. “I guess I wanted to stretch my wings,” she added and lowered to the ground.

The Street Surgeon Team paused during this incident.

Imonary gestured to everyone to stay put. “We’re not in the notorious forest of Swamp Nation of Moonsteep,” he reminded the group,”all of you experienced a year living within Swamp Nation, to prepare for this mission. Kidney, wipe that smirk off your face, because you are not at home,” he ordered shaking a finger in the face of the monster Street Surgeon.

Kidney obeyed to order.

Sheranda exchanged expressions with her colleagues.

"We need to creep into Lucifer City, but first we're trudging through this quarrelsome forest to hide from sinister forces. Greenie Beanie Jeanie is a Zerth person and she told all of you before we departed from the Amb-Lance this would require all of us all our senses and our common sense. We are here on Zerth to rescue, to bring home Fire Knights held hostage in an illegal medical facility," he added.

"Many of my people perished collecting this information," Greenie Beanie Jeanie spoke up.

The Street Surgeons exchanged expressions.

"We work as a virus, an organism, and the function of a virus is to survive by leeching off the host, so as Street Surgeons we survive the jungle by respecting the host. Be alert," Pulmonary encouraged.

Squadron Leader gestured to everyone to keep following.

Kidney decided to activate the Cyclops goggle eye lens to infrared. "*I am not going to be a victim in these woods, become a picnic for weird creatures*," he thought and turning to Sheranda to copycat his actions. She scrunched her face showing puzzlement.

"*I have known Kidney since our time at Hammurabi Medical University, he would never navigate me into danger*," she thought and nodding reaching down to the utility belt and withdrew the Street Surgeon Mahagick goggles covering both eyes. "*Kidney's*

Bloodline is a big influence in Swamp Nation and he is one three Fungus members to ever achieve membership in the Hammurabi University, a natural born care giver," she continued thinking.

Two hours later.

Deeper into the wild untamed world of shrieking sounds.

Kidney and Sheranda stepped upon the layered foliage of twigs, clumps of meter tall horn grass. Moisture within the soil oozed where they stepped. On their feet were designated Trudge Boots. The gloves protected them from razor sharp bites from Clawsquitoes. The superior fabric could be penetrated. And the Tarantula-Hoppers add another level of danger. All the equipment for Street Surgeons was invented by the Mahagick Corporation.

Sheranda swatted at the Tarantula-Hoppers with either her hand or a swish of a wing. "*Always maintain calmness,*" she told herself. It was an instinctive self-defence maneuver. It could be overwhelming with the wild untamed environment. But, it would also shake off any additional Tarantula-Hoppers that might be clinging to the feathers of her wings. Kidney watched as many as ten critters were immediately shaken off onto the ground and Squadron Leader performed the same mode of defence. Once off the wings they hopped away. She lowered and landed one by accident squeezing its guts out. It was not deliberate, clumsy, and she shook her head. Kidney smirked responding to the incident.

Fifteen minutes later.

A layer of jungle mist acted as a thick stage curtain, and the Squadron Leader gestured to everyone stand still. She gestured to Team Leader Pulmonary to use the Mahagick goggles and scan the immediate surroundings. The Street Surgeons followed her silent order.

"We don't want to provoke any large forest beasts," Pulmonary deadpanned.

"We'll punch Tarantula-Hoppers," Salvo replied punching away two with a left hook and a right forward punch. "My phobia is really getting under my skin," he admitted.

"Street Surgeons are not supposed to have phobias," Sheranda scolded, but in playful manner.

Kidney adjusted the scanning system of the single lens by tapping buttons on the Street Surgeon belt buckle. The information was wirelessly transmitted. The lens zoomed so objects far away could be seen close up. The system also sliced through the mist and captured moving images.

"Dumb-Bats," he muttered.

"Dumb-Bats," Salvo spoke up.

"Move ahead," Squadron Leader encouraged giving a hand signal to proceed.

"Dumb-Bats can be -domes domesticated," Pulmonary replied as he sensed a trickling of sensation through his bones. "Dumb-Bats – are our friend," he added controlling his fear by keeping releasing his breathing slow and steady. His vocal cords were a little tight. He had trained himself over many decades to control his emotional intelligence.

"I see a stone bridge," Kidney said amused. He could hear Pulmonary's voice trip.

"No, that's not a bridge, it's Zerth ancient art," Pulmonary deadpanned.

"I cannot see any danger lurking," Sheranda spoke up. "*Go to flight mode, silly*," she thought and again spontaneously lifted to the height of five meters.

Squadron Leader responded to Sheranda. Their wings held them in hover mode. She needed to get above the jungle and gestured a wee bit higher and so together they held hands, something Dewskinners learn in their Nooner Years of flight training, a traditional buddy system. They gracefully flapped their wings and moved up additional ten meters. The could see no harm and landed.

"No Moshekeeduus," Squadron Leader reported.

"Vile and evil creatures," Greenie Beanie Jeanie remarked. "One those creatures almost injured my Dad, and my Mom used the Zapper Pistol to kill one," she explained. "This happened before the most traumatic incident in my life gave way to a new path," she added.

The other cast expressions upon a woman older than themselves. Greenie dgdfgdg\dgeanie stood no taller than four feet five inches, but she was a fully trained Fire Knight and trained by a man.

The graduate students followed the mentors through the mist and could not help but nearly taste the odor. It was trapped within the mist, piquant aroma. Gradually the lift thinned and the group arrived in an outcropping next to the stone bridge spanning a gorge.

Lee-Lee Southfly and Prince Sherrout exchanged expressions. Sherrout's wore a fish bowl over his head with pipe cleaner inside and eyeballs on top. It was transparent liquid. The expressions of his eyes reflected his inner emotions. Lee-Lee Southfly nodded accepting the wide-eyed expression language. Prince Sherrout rolled his eyes.

"Scaredee-cat!" he spoke.

"The bridge is covered with Dumb-Bats," Salvo remarked stopping mid-stride.

Prince Sherrout ran onto the bridge waving his arms and halted after twenty feet.

The Dumb-Bats were taken by surprise. Quickly they leaped off the edges of the bridge giving off quirky sounds, not amused.

"Very dumb," Squadron Leader remarked.

"Just a silly joke."

Squadron Leader gestured to Sheranda to go to flight and to follow. "Let's check to see if this bridge will hold up for us, so we can cross it," she commented. And so they flew underneath checking the thickness.

"*Truly a remarkable ancient age of marvellous technology, a cobblestone bridge in the sky. It must be one of the unknown wonders of planet Zerth,*" Sheranda thought. "*It must have been built a race other than Enoch or the Befour Nation,*" she continued thinking. She saw her mentor, Kayla, gesture to land back on the bridge.

"The Nayam Tribe once numbered seventeen million," Salvo said, "and they are responsible for many stone age buildings, temples," he explained. "In what can be only described as a pandemic, after more than twelve centuries of living, devoting themselves to their gods, the Nayam Tribe was wiped off Zerth in less than five years," he continued.

"So true," Greenie Beanie Jeanie agreed.

"So depressing," Sherrout said.

"We only tell happy stories," Lee-Lee Southfly insisted confront his colleague and deliberately pushing a single finger into his upper chest. "Happy stories."he repeated.

Salvo shrugged. "Sssssorrry." Suddenly he ducked avoiding colliding with several sparrow size and swift moving Dumb-Bats.

The Street Surgeons all fell about, either to the knees or crouching as dozens more sparrow-size Dumb-Bats zoomed toward them. The creatures had eight inch long serpent whip-tails, but did not attack the Street Surgeons, who covered their heads in reaction. The winged Dumb-Bats were natural skilled aviators of the sky as any human pilot will claim they perform acrobatics agility with supernatural ability.

And to show off, five Dumb-Bats one at a time landed upon Salvo's knapsack and leaped off resuming flight as if the creatures required a springboard. When he stood up he could see other exchanging expressions, giving him various gestures, "Bravo... So cool... You're the man... Oh, the Dumb-Bats love you, a real charmer!" It was all said in good nature, but Salvo quivered nervously. "But I am not a Dumb-Bat!"

"Awesome display of aviator skills," Sheranda teased. "My Father, Commander Cyrano Hammurabi is a Comet Chaser Platoon as I have told all of many times. He has studied how the sparrow-size Dumb-Bats fly and admits if had just one hundred Dumb-Bats they would become the orchestra aviators, flawless and thus runaway comets or asteroids would not stand a chance of crashing into a planet or celestial body, a moon," she added and giggled amusing herself.

"Keep moving," Pulmonary ordered. "Dumb-Bats don't bite unless they really, really feel fear and those whip-tails are strategic weapons of defence," he added.

"Dumb-Bats are the chosen bird by Great Spirit," Greenie Beanie Jeanie said.

"According to the Great Spirit Book, Dumb-Bats can break the sound barrier," Sheranda remarked, "if they truly to go war with an enemy creature goes on attack mode," she added.

Thousands of Dumb-Bats suddenly filled the sky while pursued by several natural predators, Zargoyls. Sheranda began dancing on the spot as the Zargoyls whizzed by on the left and right pursuing the Dumb-Bats. She lost her footing twisting around and around and crouching to protect herself she slipped and fell backwards over the edge of the ancient stone bridge.

"Sheranda!" Salvo and Greenie Beanie Jeanie and Frequent Sea Seven shouted in horror.

Squadron Leader and Pulmonary gestured to settle down.

The Zargoyls and Dumb-Bats cleared the area, flying off into horizon.

Greenie Beanie Jeanie was first and foremost a train Fire Knight and only recently signed up to the Moonsteep Medical Empire to get more medical training. People who knew her well enough had an expression, “Four foot five inch of total determination, the bulldozer!”... The green skin natural pigment on Zerth for her race, but orange was another colour distinct for Zerthlings. She was the eldest person in the current group, but her DNA hid her true wrinkles keeping youthful, considered a 5-Olympia measurement complete with her Fire Knight skills. She was the most dangerous person in the troop. She got her education and training on earth 34567 at Fire Knight Academy located in Abraham State in Canamerica.

Sheranda whooshed back up like a ball bouncing off a wall and hovered for a few seconds before touching down. Greenie immediately flung open her arms embracing her friend.

“Don’t ever scare me to death like that again!” she scolded.

“I am Dewskinner, Befour Nation person and I therefore my race like Squadron Leader have wings,” Sheranda replied exchanging a hug. “And you are wrinkling my feathers,” she added with a twist of wit.

Greenie let go and stepped back. She cleared her dry throat. “Sorry to show affection, I was overwhelmed,” she said.

“Short-Stop, you overwhelm me,” Sheranda replied calling her a nickname.

“I played baseball as a kid and my short stature and youthful appearance only makes me resemble a teenager, but I am over two hundred years old,” Greenie said resuming a monotone voice.

“Let’s get clear off the Nayam Bridge,” Pulmonary insisted.

The Street Surgeons continued trudging through the forest making a path as they went along. Pulmonary frequently checked the compass keeping the troop in the direction they needed to go.

“We’re walking in circles!” Frequency Sea-Seven spoke releasing inner frustration.

“No we are not walking in circle,” Pulmonary defended himself.

“Quiet, everyone,” Kidney shouted a command. He raised his nose in the air and sniffed. “I smell an odor lingering not far,” he said.

Bursting through the tall shrubs forming vertical strips drapes came three open mouth slobbering creature. The oily protected it because it had no hair covering its body. Clawsquitoes and

Tarantula-Hoppers and other insects biting on the naked skin. The oil acted a defence killing off insects.

"Moshskeeduus!" Greenie exclaimed and quickly reaching behind back and removing from the sheath an Evergreen Phyresword. Pressing a button and the primordial element Phyre sprang up into an incandescent green flame. And with her Fire Knight training skills over the years, she needed now. She swiftly moved in battle mode raising the Phyresword clutching the grip handle with two hands. She took up a classic battle stance, stretching one leg forward and placing her other leg sideways and a foot pointed outward. Performing a standard downward cut maneuver and the Mahagick power of the Phyreblade sliced clean through the arm of the first Moshskeeduu. It released a shrieking and painful scream clutching the wound and running off scared. "Two more," Greenie said.

"Don't touch the skin, the oil it excretes will burn your hand!" Kidney said speaking an agitated tone and simultaneously pulling Salvo out of harm's way.

Sheranda reached forward gabbing her zebra striped girlfriend, Frequent Sea Seven, an Eknakamoonknoon person, under the armpits. The wings spread open wide and lifting herself and her girlfriend out of the danger zone.

Frequent Sea Seven gave a hearty angry shout before kicking a foot forward and the boot heel smacked a Moshskeeduu smack-dab in the forehead. The creature was jarred backwards, but it was not knocked off the its feet.

“Not so high. Sheranda, you know I hate heights!”

“Quiet, you are in my hands.”

Swinging the Evergreen Phyresword, Greenie aimed the primordial energy at one of the two remaining Moshskeeduus as one lunged at her. The claw paws were out stretched ready to tear through her skin. She responded with a sequence of blows and each time slicing the Moshskeeduu and each slice opened gaps in the extended arms, chest and finally the legs. It began squirting blood. The final slice was done at lightning speed across the throat and it dropped, flopped over started convulsing.

The last Moshskeeduu grabbed Greenie from around the torso picking her up like it had just won a prize. Pulmonary did not hesitate firing continuously using the Mahagick Pistol. Energy bolts repetitively punched the Moshskeeduu knocking it back until it fell off the cliff side screaming all the way down the gorge.

Private Thoughts

"*Sierrahotelcholromeoalphanovermberdeltaaphasierr atangooscaruniformdeltunformpapfoxrotoscarrmkeechop apahoelscarromeoalphanovermebertagoechdetla – fight foxtrotindiagolftangobravotangowlimalimaindiaechosier re*," Kidney thought thinking in his indigenous Talloween language.

Dead Soul Road

Current Time 11:07 a.m.

The lingering funk odor was obnoxiously unpleasant to the nose.

"Audacious!" Kidney said as the Street Surgeon Troop emerged from the jungle onto a single dirt road. He made a face. "My older brother plays music from his butt cheeks and it's stinky," he added attempting to be funny, but received various facial expressions.

"Your humour, it's pure punishment," Pulmonary deadpanned. "But if you wish to date a single girl skunk, be my guest," he added.

"This is known as Dead Soul Road, the backside of Lucifer City," Greenie remarked in a casual tone making a gesture. "Dead Soul Road has been here since rein of King Baal and you can tell it has never eroded because the asphalt is not asphalt as by conventional science. The ancient people, the Nayam Tribe built this road harnessing Psyance, a major compartmentalized branch of Mahagick. It's comprised of Mahagick Primordial Element making is indestructible, erosion proof, but weeds can crawl across the surface, smother it like a blanket and protect it from those who may try to chip a piece off and understand the secrets hidden in the stone," she explained.

"How did the Nayam Tribe learn about Mahagick-Psyance?"

Sheranda asked.

Greenie shrugged.

Kidney spotted red dome weeds seeing how the head bobbled in the subtle breeze. He walked over kneeling observing the batch with keen interest, "*Whiskeyechohotelscarromeofoxtrotlimaoscarwhiskeyromeo*," he thought rubbing his chin curious. He withdrew a small round plastic container from his utility and twisted off the cap. Next, he plucked five weeds, which included the roots, and pushed the clump inside container and put the cap back on and again slipped it back inside a utility pocket.

"You like plants," Squadron Leader teased.

"As a Swamp Nation person, plants are our biggest resource for medical study," Kidney replied in a teaching manner. He gave a nod as a polite bow to his superior.

"You're smart," she said in a confident tone.

"Be humble, be patient and be willing to learn," Kidney replied.

"Collecting weeds today," Pulmonary deadpanned, "and tomorrow it will be frogs," he continued.

"I think Zogs are much more attractive thank mere hopping frogs, thanks for the suggestion," Kidney replied.

Greenie quickly stepped forward confronting the situation. “Ahem!” she cleared her throat. “Team Leader, Squadron Leader, let me introduce the plant Kidney just plucked. These woolly red dome are part of the Weeflower family, this particular ones are called, Zandee’Nylons. In total there are six types of Weeflowers scattered across the known Twelve Zodiac Multiverse,” she explained.

“Zandee’Nylons,” Frequency Sea Seven repeated fascinated by Kidney’s actions. “Extremely cool.”

“Okay, let’s push on, we need get to Fire Knight Forte,” Pulmonary spoke up.

Greenie nodded agreeing. “Spirit-Phyre is one of Twelve Primordial Gods and according to the Great Spirit Book he nearly killed off all the Zandee’Nylons in a fit of rage. Great Gwen Spirit refused to let Spirit-Phyre guard the Primordial Treasure because it was her treasure. She did not want to share her treasure of Primordial Elements. And then Spirit-Phyre turned on his sister and assisted Arezon-Knysght during the Primordial Battle of Taprobane Island. To protect the seeds, Great Spirit scatted the seeds across the Twelve Zodiac Multiverses. The weeds can provide Mahagick serums,” she explained.

“Greenie, you spin a yarn, a history lesson and a storyteller,” Squadron Leader complimented.

“I wish I had you telling me bedtime stories,” Prince Sherrout said.

Bloodlines or Cloning?

The Street Surgeons walked along Dead Soul Road, which a twenty-five foot high rock wall topped with barbwire ran alongside it. The rock wall was the same type of stone the Nayam Tribe used for the road, indestructible and Greenie told her friends the Tribe had built the rock wall encompassing the eight percent of what is modern day Lucifer City.

"What was the original name?" Sheranda asked.

"Bethlehem."

"Never heard of it," Lee-Lee South fly admitted.

Greenie gazed upward at the sky hearing a flock of birds squawking overhead. "In school, in my home town of Spirit of Seven Cowboys, I visited Lucifer City with some friends. All of us played hookie from school and my friends invited me a rock show. I was fourteen at the time," she said.

"Bethlehem is one of the most ancient 'words' in history," Squadron Leader remarked while flexing her wings, stretching them and then folding them against her backside.

"This city has had a lot of names attached to it," Greenie said.

"What are others names?" Prince Sherrout asked intrigued.

"Lucifer City, before King Baal conquered it, stealing it away from Anubis Shoal, the soul catcher of planet Zerth, it was Anubis who ruled this vast region. Meanwhile, King Baal was on his adventures making war on Taprobane Island under his warrior name, Arezon-Knysght. Anubis was not a warrior/ king, he inherited the city from his Father, King Shoal and even shocked his Father when he decided to rebuild the infrastructure that had been eroding for decades. And so, Prince Anubis and his Bloodline of seven sons passionately had the people rebuild the city and rather being a tyrant, gave the people beautiful homes and spas and all the fine things hard working people could dream. He cultivated the best farmers and food supply chains including lumber and brick supply chains. He was a wizard, not a warrior, a simple prince for the people and going against his Father, King Shoal, Prince Shoal gave the people of Bethlehem, one month 'no tax' and food, clothing everything, one single month," Greenie explained.

"What happen, did everyone live happily ever after?" Kidney asked.

"And then reality set it, upon returning home from Taprobane Island, King Baal, now a brutal warlord, Arezon-Knysght, captured Lucifer City in a single Zerth day and slit the throat of King Shoal, plucked out his eyeballs, cut of each digit of his fingers and then hung him from the rafters over a bathtub. It is rumoured, Arezon-Knysght bathed in his blood, a shower. And Queen Shoal, he engaged in sex with her corpse, and slept with it for several days before tossing her body into a pile of other bodies and bones of those who attempted to stop him from conquering the city. The person known as King Baal became Arezon-Knysght, as it was foretold in Great Spirit Book," Greenie said.

"Not cool," Sheranda replied.

"What else can you tell us about King Baal?" Frequent Sea Seven asked.

"Conjecture on specific dates, Anubis was born Before the Common Era according the Zerth Timeline. King Baal was born in 1670 in the Calendar Year Mytika, named after one of the old gods. Baal was one of thirty-five males to named Baal, a Bloodline stretching further back than Anubis and conjecture claims he not human, something else, otherworldly, because he prayed to an unknown classic god, Amemga," Greenie said. "It was Baal number thirty-two who attempted to capture Great Spirit Temple on Taprobane Island, drastically failed, but then turned around and conquered Bethlehem in a single day," she said.

"Planet Zerth had experienced horrible things, since the satellite Shadow-Face was struck by a rogue asteroid shattering it. Fragments destroyed a world, billions dead, a handful of survivors," Salvo commented.

Frequency Sea Seven

"All the thirty-two males were named, Baal, sounds crummy," Frequency Sea Seven said. The facial epidermis shift from zebra stripes to an all-creamy ivory and them smoothly shifted to all-raven. Mentally she controlled the facial epidermis finally selecting a hue she could feel comfortable. "It sounds like experimental cloning, Baal model one, two, three, so on and so on," she continued. Next, she began mentally manipulate her shoulder length hair causing it to become a bun. Frequency performed this activity daily to keep the muscle reflex in shape. Suddenly the bun wrapped itself so quickly and it stretch out, ***Snap! Snap! Snap!*** It stretch to a full length of one hundred feet in less than five seconds. She cracked it like a whip and then it spun itself back up into a bun.

"Cloning, I never imagined that before," Greenie admitted intrigued by how fast Frequency Sea Seven caught on. "As a Zerth person, there are rumours of ancient experiments performed on people abducted by the gods," she added. "I had an uncle who claimed he was taken away, somewhere and returned," she said while continue to stroll along Dead Soul Road.

"Amemga were abducting members of the Nayam Tribe, intriguing," Kidney said. "Be humble, be patient and be willing to learn," he added.

"It's a myth all knowledge comes from Afar, a forgotten or dead universe," Prince Sherrout pointed out. "My own Manlantean race spawned a seed on an earth-like world and those people were given the name, Atlanteans," he explained.

"Here we are, Fire Knight Forte," Greenie said.

Greenie's Story

The Street Surgeons arrived at a brick wall and stood stumped with the exception of Greenie.

"I don't see a back door?" Sheranda admitted as her wings stretched and folded back loosely.

Greenie responded with a sly smile. "The warehouse is a fortress built long ago for the original Fire Knights. One of those original Fire Knights was a Mahagick Member, Michelle Mercury, a Murian and all Murians are categorized as Supernaturals. Michelle harnessed Mahagick Elements and conjured up a fortress which resembles a warehouse. I learned this history lesson from my mentor, Simon Knight and Simon was truly Fire Knight and he had a weird relationship with Mercury. I earned my training to become a Fire Knight on earth 34567 at the famous Fire Knight Academy and after accomplishing that I decided to double down to learn more about medicine at the Hammurabi Medical Center to become an associate with Street Surgeons," Greenie explained.

"And how was your relationship with Simon Knight?" Squadron Leader asked a specific question knowing in advance some medical information about Greenie. As Squadron Leader, it was her responsibility to know about the team players of the Street Surgeons, otherwise Greenie would be disqualified.

"Simon eventually replaced my Father and Mercury became a replacement for my Mother, and I found some happiness. My parents were murdered, cold, ice cold, and I found them in bed after I had broken curfew, skipped school with friends and the murderers never found. Simon Knight and the Fire Knight Troop he was associated with came to my rescue," Greenie said.

"Any regrets?" Squadron Leader asked.

"Travelling to Lucifer City as a teenager with friends to see a stupid rock concert, The Super Assassins."

"But had you been at home on that fateful day --"

Greenie interrupted. She released a tone of agitation mixed with anger. "The murderers of parents would certainly have done the action towards me," she stated in a matter of fact tone. "Simon and Mercury, we've spoken about how fate dragged me with my friends and returned me home for me to find my parents in bed, bloody and very dead," she continued. "No child should discover their parents dead and I have often asked Great Spirit why 'me'? I keep receiving the same message in my head," she confessed.

"What message?" Squadron Leader asked.

"Be humble, be patient and be willing to learn," Greenie replied.

"I like expression, Great Spirit wrote that," Kidney said.

"Simon Knight got classified as a Superhero because of the DNA gene thirteen. He's my height, five feet. Don't let his height fool you, expert in weapons and hand-to-hand combat and smart," Greenie said.

"My Father introduced me to Fire Knights when we visited earth 34567, a business trip for my Father. And my Mother also had business with the Fire Knight Moonsteep Hospital," Sheranda remarked.

"Where is the door?" Prince Sherrout asked.

"I don't see a door," Lee-Lee- Southfly commented.

"Let's search for the door," Kidney suggested raising a brow and steering the conversation. He rubbed the left side of his nostril sensing the piquant odor.

Squadron Leader wrapped Greenie in her wings in a girlfriend embrace, and after a moment released her teammate.

"Oh! Right! The door!" Greenie stepped forward emerging from wings with two broad strides perhaps like with the energy of a child, excited. She faced the brick wall. She clapped producing a unique sound wave.

Everyone watched wondering Greenie was doing.

Salvo and Sherrout decided to applaud and this encouraged Sheranda and Kidney to copycat them and then Lee-Lee Southfly and Frequency.

Greenie turned around sharing a smart-aleck expression.

Pulmonary decided to merely give a two thumbs-up gesture.

Squadron Leader cast an expression at all them and sighed.

The Zerth Fire Knight Fort

A glitter of purple energy transformed forming a rectangle. A portion of the brick wall mutated take the shape of a door and it was swung open welcoming the next guests. Greenie gestured to follow.

Kidney's cyclops eye scanned the main floor seeing a medieval knight statue standing next to a fireplace. To the left was a large wooden round table with modern office styled swivel high-back chairs with wheels. The kitchen was further back, in another room through an open arching entrance. The single goggle lens adjusted according the 'light density'. His single eye fell upon the Fire Knight Shield hanging on a wall showing images for symbols, the Griffin, and the energy known as Merkaba and the Evergreen Phyresword. Oil portraits of Fire Knights hung on the surrounding walls and each person was given distinct quirky facing expressions by the painter. Rubbing his cheeks with his thumb and index-finger in thoughtful manner he was captured by how the painter had done his job, making the Fire Knights life like. Looking up he saw thick wooden beams holding up a second floor and light bulbs containing blue Zilohertz crystals gave off light. His eyes moved scanning seeing the staircase going up in a switchback style and at the top was the second floor. Raising his nose in the air he could smell a scent, something he recognized, musk, but not overpowering. "

Sierrayankeenovermbertangohotelechotangoindiacharliesierra charlieechonovemeber," he thought.

"Oh! Cool!" Lee-Lee Southfly exclaimed pointing.

"It's a fireman's pole!" Sheranda said with glee catching Kidney's attention. "A fireman's pole!" She pointed.

"The pole is not for dancing," Pulmonary said as he touched the it and then jumped in the air and swung around it to amuse the troop. "OK, enough drama," he remarked.

"The pole is connected to the sleeping chamber," Greenie said. "I lived here with my mentor, Simon-Knight and the members of the Fire Knight Troop for three years before travelling to Fire Knight Castle on earth 34567," she explained.

"I am going up stairs," Salvo said hurrying toward the staircase, "I gotta try this pole." And up the stairs he rushed and a few minutes later slid down it and landed squarely on his butt. "Owe!"

Everyone laughed.

"You're a Street Surgeon, Salvo, not a Fire Knight," Greenie teased and extended a hand helping him onto his feet.

Squadron Leader Kayla snapped her fingers three times to draw attention toward her. She gestured to gather around. The Street Surgeons formed a circle with her in the middle. "Everyone, we will spend a single night at the Fire Knight Fort thanks to Greenie. Open your knapsacks, remove all the food packs and spread the food on the table because all us will require a good dinner after such a long jungle trek. We will also require a breakfast before engaging in our mission activities, which is to rescue trapped Fire Knights inside Lucifer City. Greenie will give us more information later, for now, let's settle in," she said. "Does anyone have anything to add?" she asked.

"Rodent!" Salvo exclaimed pointing. He jumped into the arms of Pulmonary quivering. "Rodent! Rodent. Shoot it!" he said.

Kidney withdrew the Mahagick pistol. Quickly he adjusted the dial setting for the one he wanted. He aimed and fired, capturing the rodent inside a cocoon. He slung the pistol back inside the holster. Kneeling, he picking up the cocoon with the rodent inside, he purposely dangled it in front of Salvo.

"Back home, this rodent would be a roasted on a Barbie-Q, but we Swamp People are little more cultured these days. I will place the specimen inside a stasis to examine it," Kidney said.

Salvo

Pulmonary released Salvo back to his feet.

Sheranda cast an unforgiving glare at Kidney. "Nkere! Zzwaa'wat dusz twa'dat ahhdeeblute?" She thought in her Befournese language.

Kidney scratched his head, puzzled. "I am what I supposed to be and as my friend you know how I like to study things," he said. Next, approaching Salvo he gave a polite nod. "You will always be my friend. Let me put the critter away so you won't be afraid of it." And Kidney withdrew again from the Street Surgeon utility belt a round disk and after pressing the centre button the Nanotech formed a transparent stasis container. Twisting off the cap he shoved the rodent inside. Pressing a side button it filled with liquid to keep it preserved.

Frequency Sea Seven stepped forward as if on cue. "Salvo, I am a trained Mind Mender, so let me linkup my mind with your neurons so I may learn about your fears," she said taking his hands inviting him closer. Her hair began to wrap around his body bringing him even closer. "I really like a tortured mind, you really make my education worth every penny," Frequent Sea Seven said.

Salvo squirmed his way free of his teammate and he zoomed behind Kidney, the bodyguard. "Don't come near me with that witchery of mind," he defended himself.

Sherrout tugged on Salvo's sleeve. "Let's get our knapsack food on the table, no need to have your mind probed," he recommended.

Frequency Sea Seven's hair again wrapped up into a bun. "I am here for you, Salvo," she said.

"Salvo," Kidney said, "the Swamp Nation has the Aspidistra plant and it's cousin is the Stradipasi plant, which can grow in nearly every conceivable environment. Great Spirit blessed the Stradipasi plant, which is good smoking. Stradipasi is nicknamed, the Virgin Plant. You and Me, we should get down and a trip together," he recommended. "Take my doctor's advice, a smoke at times is worthy to release the mind, fly off to another dimension," he said.

"I liked the taste of Stradipasi," Sheranda replied with a smile.

"This mission is for only the insane," Salvo quipped.

"I need a second opinion on that issue," Frequent Sea Seven teased as she pulled the slipknot on the knapsack.

"Why is the Stradipasi is nicknamed, the Virgin Plant?" Pulmonary asked.

"Smoke it, and go visit Great Spirit!" Kidney replied with a quirky punchline.

Pulmonary and Squadron Leader exchanged expressions and then release a chortle.

Dinner Talk

The Street Surgeon Troop sitting the Fire Knight round table with food assorted packages grouped together. It was protein food specifically designed for a mission off-world, developed by the Moonsteep Medical Empire in association with Mahagick Food Company. The knapsacks containing food could easily one hundred people. Soup packages, high energy bars, crunchy Moonachos, assorted crackers, flavoured cream cheese contained in a toothpaste container, Yogourts, Doodle-Fruity soups, dry splotchy vegetables and salt and sweet nature bars, orange juice candy, apple fruit candy, grapefruit candy and pink lemonade candy. Food which needed to be warmed up was done so by using the Mahagick Pan, created by the Mahagick Department harnessing Mahagick Psyance.

"Impeccable," Prince Sherrout said as his eyeballs looked through the transparent fishbowl over his head. The eyes appeared to be magnified, larger than actually were, which would make children laugh. The pipe-cleaner nerves attached to the eyeballs pulsated with inner life force. And his actual brain was covered in a strange Brainstorm Cloud, a Moonsteep medical term and always keeping it shrouded and protected, but it too pulsated with life force energy.

"Sherrout, a feat for a Prince," Kidney remarked giving his friendly slap on both shoulders before sitting next to Salvo. They traded a thumb-touch.

"A feast should be for the hungry. I am Prince of my Manlantean people, but my brother is to be king one day, and so that gave me opportunity to enter the Moonsteep Medical Services," he replied. "I am fortunate to earn the rank of a Street Surgeon. My Father, King Sturgeon, at first was baffled why I would attempt becoming a medical professional, but he did not thwart my goal and over the years I impressed him with my stats. My Father says I take after my Mother, the physician he ultimately married, and she claims he is crankiest, sour-puss and quirkiest patient on Moonsteep," he added with a humble witty attitude.

Everyone chuckled.

"And so now we know why you are so cranky, sour-puss and quirkiest patient," Squadron Leader pointed. "Before we set upon this mission, you gave every excuse under the sun not be examined by Kidney Fungus --."

Kidney interrupted agitated. "And including citing a Hammurabi Medical Verse, 'No examination of a nobleman can be exercised without expression written by the King', and your King Sturgeon – Father agreed'! But you did not realize I exercised my Medical Rite and cited clause, 'A nobleman can be examined if the medical community deems that a nobleman is abusing his power'. Gotcha!" Kidney gave a big cheesy smile.

Sherrout released a big laugh blushing and nodding his head. "*Busted*!" he thought. "It seems I inherited my Mother's brains and a mixture of my Father's attitude, a strange Molotov Cocktail, just don't fruit juice, it might cure the common cold," he teased. "You are very clever and manipulative," he added with a change of tone.

Kidney nodded in a humble manner. "I love a patient that has a some fight," he explained. "It gives me boxing practice metaphorically," he added.

"On a couple of occasions, "I have to harness my Zerth super duper strength and manhandle patients," Greenie commented.

"Manhandle?" Troop Leader Pulmonary asked.

"I witnessed Greenie pick a sumo wrestle up off his feet and over her head and carry him down hall and slam him back in his bed and then strap him down to the bed," Sheranda said. "Short-Stop pulls out all the stops when it comes to controlling impatient patients," she added calling her friend an affectionate nickname.

"The sumo wrestler called me, Little Mother, after that incident and behaved himself, sort of," Greenie remarked.

"How did you develop your phobia, Salvo?" Frequent Sea Seven asked steering the conversation. "The Moonsteep Medical Empire does not accept ableism. Our goal is to work with people with physical or mental issues," she remarked.

"Agender," Sheranda snapped up a comment. "As a Street Surgeon we are blind to all genders, races, religion and those who hate," she said as the Teammates nodded in agreement.

The Aquaskin Moonsteep person spoke with hand gestures as part of his culture. The quirky sign language was incorporated from childhood, although he speak fluently in several physical languages, but sign language had developed across Moonsteep into a single language so all who learned it could speak to someone in another country without an interpreter. The man who invented the universally language, his last name was Sign, Dr. Thumb Sign and he too was Aquaskin person.

Salvo had no need for a shirt because his sculptured body physique naturally produced a supernatural warmth, something girls would be attracted to as it emitted a little pheromone for attraction. He had a seventy-two inch and creamy green coloured chest. The Aquaskin epidermis could absorb sunlight transforming through osmosis energy, combining it with photosynthesis, and thus his race was partially plant organic and so that's why Salvo shaved his leafy under armpits and trimmed his head of sea weed. He never cut the thin sea weed ponytail as it was part of his culture, but it tied knots. Currently the ponytail had fifty five knots and sat comfortably shoulder length.

"Phobias are an inner warfare of the mind," Lee-Lee Southfly spoke up. “Phobias attack the mind where often it becomes a nerve wracking episode people endure throughout their lives,” he added while selecting the Doodle-Fruit soup to eat.

“How would you understand about Phobias?” Frequent Sea Seven asked.

“Phobia Class; studying causes of phobias and over coming them was my undergraduate,” Lee-Lee Southfly said. “Antibiotics won’t cure a phobia,” he added.

“Anyone want to buy a phobia?” Pulmonary deadpanned.

“My phobia is keraunophobia.”

“Noise,” Sheranda said and bit down on the Moonacho smothered with salad dripping dressing. ***Crunch!***

“I also don’t like ornithophobia,” Salvo admitted. “And ailurophobia,” he admitted.

“I am losing count,” Greenie said.

“Cats,” Frequent Sea Seven asked while using he hair to grasp a spoon to scoop yogourt out and feed herself. She manipulated her hair just like using a third hand! “But you once told me you had adopted two large Ber-Ku cats,” she remarked.

“Psychology, to teach myself to get over the fear of cats,” Salvo said. “And at night I use a knight light,” he added.

“Me to,” Prince Sherrout squeaked.

“Count me in, I really, really, really dread the dark,” Pulmonary said raising his hand. He was eating a power bar of sweet apple and nuts.

“What’s your phobia, Kayla?” Kidney asked.

“Uhhh, me?” the Squadron Leader asked surprised. “I am not allowed to have a phobia, my profession demands of me to teach graduate students to improve Street Surgeon skills,” she asserted.

“The topic at the table is PHOBIA, and we should discuss it,” Kidney remarked.

“What is your phobia?”

Kidney stood up and slammed a palm on the table. Items jumped. “Squadron Leader, I asked you first,” he insisted. “We are a team. And as teammates we learn from one other our weaknesses and how to overcome them which will make up mentally stronger through working on solutions and survive situations we cannot predict,” he said.

“Lightning is an honest phobia,” Sheranda said.

“Vertigo, fear of heights,” Pulmonary agreed.

"Bugs, insects," Frequent Sea Seven said finishing the yogourt. She manipulated her hair to lower the spoon carefully onto the place. Next, her hair stretched out and dropped the empty container into an open kitchen garbage can.

"Touch can be an honest phobia," Lee-Lee Southfly said. "The epidermis is our first sensory input through the physical form of touch, soft, harsh, gritty, slime, cold or hot and/ or uninvited touching and how we respond in body language through touching," he continued.

"Death is an honest phobia," Greenie Beanie Jeanie remarked. "Through death, seeing death, discovering death, and so we can be reborn, given a purpose by Great Spirit," she added.

Everyone fell silent and turned their heads curiously toward the Fire Knight trained member, but also specializing in medical training. Their friend spoke of a subject no one wanted to imagine, death.

"I had a near-death experience," Squadron Leader admitted while holding a cup of hot liquid, "when I first became a Street Surgeon," she said.

A Near-Death Experience

"Teenworld," Squadron Leader Kayla began, "a secret place all wrapped up shrouded by a fog cloud in Exotic Space. And we know Exotic Space is utterly weird compared to Outer Space, but the two are vastly different than the other, one connects universes and the other is a singular UN-I-Verse. Stranger than fiction, is the expression. Moonsteep exists in its personal UN-I-Verse, but now we're here on Zerth, which is another UN-I-Verse. Stranger than fiction... It can be confusing... And legends manifested by hardcore Exotic Sailors claim the fog cloud is a distortion of Exotic Primordial Elements or Energy or EPEs, a fabric or blanket woven by Great Spirit as a celestial quilt to keep prying eyes away from a place she had held secretive, close to her heart... But I guess after what happened during my time her heart must have been extremely heavy... Whatever. Anyway, myself and my teammates, were assigned to care for a world at war, but the world composed of teens, Classified as Immortal Teens or I.Ts which is utterly obnoxiously weird. Teenworld is a flat earth, a chunk of a perfect square rock, which truly amazing because it does not follow a star, and I cannot recall if there was a star, but it had day and night. Teenworld is situated on a perfect fixed point in Exotic Space and placed there by Great Spirit.

My Moonsteep Street Surgeon Team arrived on Teenworld, a world nicknamed, No Man's Land, given by Warlord Adolf and his Nazi Henchmen: No Man's Land because no one ever wanted to claim it, a world of ageless teenagers, Twenteeteen, thirteeteen, and fifteeteen, excreta. They wore a specific Teen Cultural clothing, nothing but top of the line. I was a Moonager same all of you, thirty-five at the time, a time spent in war. This was abomination, on one's feet from day one: repairing broken arms, legs, repairing arteries, build new brains, helped three pregnant people and that was just first six hours. I spent twelve years helping mending the wounded on Teenworld. Our Squadron Leader, and Team Leader, established a secret base deep underground in an ancient part of a city called, Skateboard... Skateboard City. It had five entrances, three inside an amusement park and two, one in the Skateboard City Library and in a farm barn. The Teenworld lived in a world of music, dance, theatre, rollerblading, sky-boarding, snowboarding, skateboarding and other teen activities.

The sky was speckled with flying fortresses suspended by giant zeppelins, but also fuelled by something called, Bitter-Juice. The smokestacks belched a stew of smoke. It stank like fried fish. They lived in a bubble-world of music, dance, theatre, rollerblading, sky-boarding, snowboarding, skateboarding and other teen activities. All that changed when Warlord Adolf invaded.

And by the time our Street Surgeon Troop arrived already two hundred and fifty thousand Teens had been rounded up by Nazi Henchmen. Me and the rest of my troop actually witnessed Nazi's using fishnets to round dozens at a time like some weird fun trap. The Teenagers were taken aboard a ship designed with these Hair Dryer style Cone Machines. They had no intention of drying a teenager's hair, but instead were using altering radio wave machines and brainwashing them becoming an agents of evil. Warlord Adolf had struck gold, a jackpot of teenage minds that could be easily altered and young enough to fill his ships with new soldiers.

I was accidentally snapped up by a fishnet during a routine Street Surgeon street sweep, our Team had found a dozen Teens in a warehouse. While members helped those teens, my Squadron Leader asked me and my teammate to do a walkabout to see others were in hiding. I was taken aboard the a ship forty-eight hours. My teammate, Bone-Marrow, a Murian and Classified as Supernatural, managed to rescue, pulling my foggy mind out of the gutter of brainwashing crap. Bone-Marrow risked his own life, sadly he died in the line of duty. He died saving my life. Murians can be killed. Murians can die. He was my best friend.

What I can say about The brainwashing Hair Dryer-Cone, it's attached to robotic arm dozens of cables stretching to the high ceiling. A person controls the robotic arm from a transparent booth, actually there are a hundred controllers and a hundred robotic arms to brainwash as a many as a hundred minds. There are men and women controllers and they were identical uniforms with an arm sleeve band displaying a twisted cross. The Hair Dryer Cone device slips over the head just around the temples and forehead. It clicks and locks in place. Radio waves at a specific frequency are beamed toward the frontal lobes and for the first fifteen minutes the sub-sonic vibrations knocks the around the lobe which starts to re-writes the sensory of the lobes, where logical decision making performed by the brain... Emotions... Rage, love, fear, sadness, hate, aggression, hunger, thirst, learning, modifying behaviour... The spectrum in all of us.

I felt I nearly died as my brain was seized my mind, but Bone-Marrow used his supernatural mental powers to release me from the radio waves. After all these years, I cannot forget that incident," Squadron Leader concluded.

Unexpected Guests

A sound attracted everyone's attention. They scrambled from the Fire Knight Table.

"My phobias toward rodents began when I was a child," Salvo said moving with the troop, "I was lying in bed. I was no more five years old. A Takkook rodent crawled up onto my leg and settled upon my stomach. My Mom discovered me and it was grandmother, and my grandmother insisted to my mother not to kill the Takkook, but to scoop it up and let it. Grandmother told me a story about the Takkook, they say it's a blessing upon an infant to befriended by a Takkook, their spirit is pure and blessed by Great Spirit," Salvo said. "That's the short version," he added.

"Shut up and put on your Street Surgeon Belt," Kidney snapped.

The Street Surgeons flew into hyperactive mode grabbing flap jackets and slipping them on. A tie string secure them. Next, they slipped on utility belts full of pockets holding precious medical supplies. They were ready to go in sixty seconds.

"I am taking the high road," Sheranda said spreading open her wings and whooshed up. She perched herself up into the rafters. She could observe the whole room. The wings folded against her back. She crouched knowing her knees were quite able to keep her steady for several hours, the bones naturally reinforced, stronger than steel, but flexible as aluminum.

Interlocking sounds produced deep hollowness as if gears were cranking counterclockwise directions. The locking sound stopped. The inside door began sliding open.

"Johnny, just hold onto to me and I will get you to the infirmary," Oriana said struggling with him. "You are blind. Your back-up pair of goggles are here in the Fire Knight Fort. You need medical attention," she continued.

First Patients

(Kickstart My Heart, Motley Crue)

Kidney swiftly moved faster than Squadron Leader and Team Leader. “Put him down!” He ordered taking Oriana by surprise.

Sheranda’s wings whooshed open like a parachute controlling her descent to the floor resembling a mighty super heroine.

Squadron Leader and Team Leader stood still watching their young Street Surgeons fly into medical mode.

“His name is Johnny Vlogger, a Fire Knight-Commander rank,” Oriana said. “And he’s not going to die on my watch!” she added. “He was born in the State of Kitty Hawk on earth 34567 in the country Canamerica. He has has dedicated his life to helping the people Zerth,” she explained.

“I know this man,” Greenie Bean Jeanie acknowledge. “Johnny Vlogger is an inspiration to everyone, a passionate toward all lifeforms. He has Troop of various people other worlds. He truly fights for people who need help. I met him just once at Fire Knight Academy, a guest lecturer in a class and my Mentor Simon-Knight arranged a meeting him and he is funny, but very smart. We talked for several hours,” she remarked.

"We found evidence of Zhoul infection," Oriana explained just the facts.

Kidney observed information the Mahagick Medical Device pop-up Holographic Screen. It showed him the anatomy. Slipping on the Mahagick Glove he touched thin-air where a button was located and switched to a different screen, zooming into microscopic level revealing blood flow.

"Salvo, Sherrout, bring a Hover-Gurney over from the Infirmary," Sheranda ordered as she leaned closer to Kidney observing the visual information. They both watched yellow arrows pointing to Nano-size oddities.

Salvo and Sherrout followed Greenie to the rear blank wall. She gestured to step back as she stood on a hopscotch pattern on the floor. The two guys exchanged expressions not seeing this pattern before. She raised her arms above her head like a ballerina and drawing in a breath. Meanwhile she started to grow taller, but truly it was her feet moving into position and finally standing on her tiptoes. She closed her eyes. She held her position harnessing energy. The two guys exchanged expressions and thumbs-up. And suddenly she began dancing with the energy of flow, not as ballerina, but a hip-hop superstar, arms moving break dancing pantomime moves while her legs cooked up a stylish symbiotic language. She had mastered the move a long time ago and the tap dancing of her feet triggered each square causing a colour flowing in rock-stomp'n rhythm and unlocking the mechanism keeping the infirmary safely guarded. Greenie stopped dancing with her feet apart on two side squares. At the conclusion of the hopscotch dance the wall slid up like a garage door.

Get your butt out of bed, bed-head

Hop to your feet, can you feel the heat of being late

School, work, church, a party

Get your butt out of bed, bed-head, feel dead?

No, you're not dead, need a shot orange juice

Hop to your feet

Hop to your feet

Don't need orange juice, I need a shot of foot stomp'n Hopscotch

Foot stomp'n Hopscotch

Get your butt out of bed, don't be such a bed-head, dead-head,

Jumping the Hopscotch will clear your foggy morning mind

Hop to your feet

Hop to your feet

Hip-hopping on those number squares, you can do it

Get your butt out of bed, don't be such a bed-head, dead-head

Grab some Hopscotch and feel your mind awaken

Hopscotch

"Greenie, stop dancing," Frequency Sea Seven said, "this is no time to show off your dance skills," she scolded.

"Quite right," Greenie agreed at bullet speed and with deadpanning zip. "Salvo, Sherrout, the Hover-Gurney is against that wall," she said pointing.

"I am Oriana, ranked as an Archer-Knight," she said, "Johnny is Mentor, Tutor and a good friend," she continued as Frequency Sea Seven approached gesturing her to settle down and taking a hold of her shaking hands.

Salvo and Sherrout returned to the main room pushing the Hover-Gurney. They pushed down on the control bar and it lowered to the floor, but still remained one inch above. A blue glow pulsated. Together they lifted and moved Johnny Vlogger Fire Knight-Commander onto the gurney.

"Knight-Commander and Myself were secretly on patrol in Lucifer City. It never surprised me the best clue to the Zhoul potion would a manufacturer in this rotten apple city. Lucifer City is no place an honest person. Our long time friend Jawbreaker, a Gartharian soldier, succumb to injuries during a fight at the Lucifer Tower Square two and a half hours ago. He died protecting us," Oriana explained speaking with nervous twitch her tone.

Frequency Sea Seven hair unwrapped itself and moved slowly down her side gradually began wrapping around Oriana. Pulling her closer in a gentle manner Freak made eye contact. "Your mind is fearful, flashes of aggression, flashes of witnessing your friend fall in battle, but our eyes are one. I am peering into your Ozone-Soul, the gift Great Spirit gave all living things. Shhhhh," she said in a soothing hypnotic tone. Oriana reached out and embraced Frequent Sea Seven.

"*UU-RR MMEL Szom'ting zboot szom'ting scribble MMEL, doughts Zzand zeets bluugy*," Sheranda thought in her Befournese language. "The yellow arrows, it's showing a virus," she remarked.

Team Leader took long strides over to the two Street Surgeons. He observed the yellow arrows.

"The M.M.D. is detecting a virus, specifically the Epiderpuss-pocket virus," Kidney concluded with a confident tone. "Epiderpuss-pocket is an air-born virus. The virus causes bodily fluids to create pockets of puss beneath the layers of skin, about a full teaspoon and the bones start absorbing the puss and they become saturated getting heavier. The rib bones push down or squeeze the lungs causing the victim unable to take regular breaths, less and less suffocating to death. The patient basically dies, lungs squeezed as tight as one can squeeze a sponge, but in this situation the sponge cannot release any juice," Kidney explained.

"The human body contains five quarts of blood, but the Epiderpuss-pocket virus will add an extra three litres," Sheranda remarked.

Squadron Leader tapped Oriana on a shoulder. "Come with me to the infirmary, you will no doubt be infected," she said as her wings stretched open and closed. Oriana could help let tears drip.

"I am in love with Johnny. He – we have spent a lot of time together, sharing assignments, but Johnny had a way of calling our assignments as 'adventures' a wise friendship," she explained.

"He is your Mentor, teacher, perhaps you both shared some closer moments and so your emotions are understood," Squadron Leader replied seeing Oriana nodding while helping over to the infirmary.

The Street Surgeon graduates took their duties inside Infirmary.

Fire Knight-Commander Vlogger was put to rest on the All-In-One Mahagick Medical Bed.

"Sheranda, I need plasma green bag, Essential-Monplasma," Kidney requested.

Sheranda searched one side of the Mahagick Med. Bed which contained several drawers each one with a symbol. Finding the correct drawer she pressed the open button and the drawer slid open revealing eight green Essential-Monplasma bags, and condensed. She yanked it out and attached it to the IV rod.

"How many drips?"

"Twenty-five drops every ten seconds," Kidney recommended.

Sheranda set in the IV-hose in Vlogger's arm. Next she set the digital switch to number of drips per second.

Frequent Sea Seven worked on patient, Oriana. She scanned using the M.M.D..

"Where does Epiderpuss-Pocket originate?" Oriana asked.

Sherrout snapped his fingers as if answering a quiz show. "Epiderpuss is from the family Epiderskinflick Group, and they include flesh eating, various skin rashes, boils and the Wrinkledermis virus, but anyway, this is just good conversation," he said.

Frequency Sea Seven nodded to herself checking the facts on the M.M.D. pop-up Holographic Screen. "Oriana, you're in excellent care. I am administering an Omni-Serum, number Seventeen to counter act any Zerth weird viruses. This booster shot will smooth over all uncomfortable headaches, perhaps ringing in your ears tummy issues and bone crunching heaviness issues." And instead of using the vials tucked inside the Street Surgeon Utility Belt, she turned to the Infirmary Omnibiotics Shelf and scanning the rows with her eyes quickly, it took a few seconds and reaching out to a vial. She disconnected it from the clamp, *snap!* Quickly she withdrew the Mahagick Medical Pistol and turning the vial upside down punctured the safe paper which then liquid filled the inner tube. Turning back to Oriana and stepping closer to the patient she pressed a finger against her chin.

"Are you nervous about me sporting a Mahagick Medical Pistol?"

Oriana responded with a grouch expression. "Just get sever pain over with, witch doctor!" she remarked.

"My pleasure, Fire Knight." Frequent Sea Seven replied grinning and it stretched because of her natural facial muscle from ear to ear. She manipulated her facial shape and for moment took the form a long-nosed wrinkle faced witch. Oriana laughed. Sea Seven pressed the flat head portion against the bicep and squeezed the trigger sending the Omni-Serum squirting out of the pistol and into the bloodstream. She returned her face to the normal Zebra image. "I perform facial fun for children, you're a big girl for me to performing for," Sea Seven added and they exchanged expressions sharing a heroine toughness.

"You keep my attention off the shot in the arm."

"Painful?"

"No paint whatsoever."

Greenie Beanie Jeanie could hear the conversation. She gave a wink to Oriana, a Fire Knight insider joke. "*Right! Fire Knights are brave souls, as so long as they scamper away from crazy doctor holding a Mahagick Pistol!*"

"But you still needed a little show," Frequent Sea Seven teased removing Omnibiotic Vial Seventeen replacing it back into the clamp, *snap!* Automatically the system unscrewed the cap so a tiny hose could refill it quickly, added another safe paper and screw the cap in place. It was completed in sixty seconds ready for use again. "I need you to strip down behind the curtain and put on the robe and when you return, stretch out on the Medic Bed. Your body requires rest. The formula will give you shivers, not bad, hurry up," she urged.

"You might have told me that before," Oriana scolded and hurried behind a curtain. She quickly started to change clothes. "I am already beginning to feel the overload of tingling in every fibre of my bones!"

"Oops, I forgot," Frequent Sea Seven remarked feeling awkward. She forced a smile. She decided to repeat the Moonsteep Medical Empire and it certainly sounded like slogan. "You're in excellent care... Oriana."

Oriana staggered out from behind the curtain. Immediately Salvo and Sherrout came along scooping her under her armpits just as she began sinking to the floor.

"No worries, we have you," Salvo said as if on cue.

"Here we go, Oriana, time for bed rest," Sherrout continued honing-in on the moment making life whimsical.

"I forgot to get Oriana to change first before I gave her the serum Omnibiotic Vial Seventeen."

"Amnesia, it could be a serious mental issue," Salvo teased scooping Oriana into arms with Sherrout to help out. They laid her on the medical bed and she quickly curled up slumbering into a passive and overdue sleep.

"Another mission successful," Sherrout said provoking a

chuckle.

The Singing Street Surgeon

Two hours later.

"The unexpected patients are sedated and serums have been administrate, they will survive," Kidney said resuming his seat at the Fire Knight table next to Sheranda. The wings bumped into him and he adjusted his body hoping not to be swatted, but too late. He stumbled backwards. Sheranda snapped out an arm and brought Kidney back upright in the chair and – plunk! "What a bad trip!" he quipped.

Everyone sat at the table.

"Focus," Squadron Leader spoke up, "Greenie Beanie Jeanie is going to layout our plans," she said.

"Lucifer City will become a mausoleum if we don't take action against the Epiderpuss-Pocket," Salvo commented.

"Epiderpuss-Pocket is a distinct Zerthling virus," Greenie pointed out, "and as Zerthling myself i have a natural immunity towards it, but I agree with Salvo, Lucifer City citizens may require a booster shot," she said.

"How many citizens reside in Lucifer City?" Lee-Lee Southfly asked.

"Seventeen million squeezed inside these tall rock walls," Team Leader Pulmonary replied. He whistled.

"Infected people untreated will be grotesque, bodies bloated, joints twisted and over time with the puss locked under the skin, clogging. The contagion has been known not just to drown people, but also explode outward from the lungs and thus spreading billions and billions of spores," Sheranda said between taking bites of a chocolate muffin.

A dish of assorted snacks sat on a plat.

"Focus," Squadron Leader spoke up again, "Greenie Beanie Jeanie is going to layout our plans," she said.

Greenie activated the Holographic Device displaying complete 360-degree image of Lucifer City. It showed animated images of people walking through the various streets, but it did not show vehicles or aircraft. Manipulating the way in which viewing the city she used wireless gloves.

"My people claim this twelve storey skyscraper is a secret Zhoul body farm, containing those secretly abducted by a sinister secret society dubbed, Soul Snatchers," Greenie began. "Long before I was born, a sweeping nation wide government program was initiated and put into law, it was known as the Zombie Worker Union. A person's Ozone-Soul could removed, harnessed inside a containment field, and then a new one could inserted into the body, and it was called Zhoul. It was a remarkable theory/ story/ a warning and told in the Great Spirit Book, the chapter **The Book About the Soul(s)**:

'Great Spirit possesses a soul she shares with a trees, weeds, whole forests and creatures in the streams interconnecting ponds and lakes and the oceans. Planets have a soul and planets that appear to be dead, they are sleeping until Great Spirit awakens them from a deep slumber. Volcanoes sleep until they are awakened and it's the same with what to appear to be dead worlds. Trees cannot grow so tall and strong enough to withstand power storms without a spirit. Forests cannot thrive without a spirit. A planet's soul is known as the Ozone soul, shielding one and all from harmful UV-B rays. The Murians possess an Ozone-Soul which makes them Supernatural. All things die and return their tiny soul to the Great Spirit and for a while remain under her wing, nurturing young spirits before setting them free again into the world in the multiverse to re-learn and re-discovering friendship, love, loneliness, and life's adventures and eventually learning about death and fight to protect life and including a fetus.

The soul is for a short time, do not attempt to master it with instruments, for the consequences of those medical actions could be contagious, irreversible, and bring forth a plague upon a world that would last the lifetime of an ocean. The soul should never be manipulated or bargained with or harnessed a weapon or even for labour. It is given freely and returned to my Great Soul upon the death of individual or thing, that is my Law of Order of Structure. No one has the wisdom, but there are those are blessed medical warriors and a handful who will only mend a wounded soul, not steal, never to steal, only to mend. I call these people my moon people.'

"When you read The Great Spirit Book, do you intentionally memorize whole segments?" Lee-Lee Southfly asked wryly.

Greenie responded with a typical Zerth expression, eyes glowing an intense green and gradually the glow simmered. "This particular twelve storey skyscraper is a secret Zhoul body farm, growing infected Zerthlings and/ or in this case perhaps the Fire Knights are obviously held against their will and cannot escape. Many of my people have suffered over the centuries, political corruption, the Law manipulated against the good people, and the cost of shelter and food. Zerth population is now at five billion and controlling that many bodies and feeding that any mouths is difficult, so the Master Controllers of Zerth are perhaps finding it difficult to contain the masses. Our target building our time to strike back at the Controllers, the Zhoul War," Greenie concluded.

"What does your people say about security?" Squadron Leader asked.

"Zilch."

"You will forgive me, but explain," Pulmonary snapped.

"It's such an ordinary building, one entrance and one exit."

"How did they get by inner security?"

"We're not going to through the front door," Frequent Sea Seven remarked.

"We are all going to rest, fun and game are past, we move into the future tomorrow," Squadron Leader instructed.

One of the Street Surgeons started humming in romantic tone. All eyes turned to Salvo at first, he was a first choice, but he pointed a finger and suddenly attention shifted to Team Leader, Pulmonary. They witnessed him singing, a Moonsteep manly romantic voice and singing to personal small toy Teddy Bear.

Street Surgeon Kidney Fungus

The kitchen light went out. The Moonsteep Street Surgeons were starting to ascend the steps to second level to sleep in the Fire Knight Quarters, with the exception of one...two.

The infirmary light illuminated. It acted a lighthouse beacon.

Kidney approached the infirmary making his way to Fire Knight Commander Johnny Vlogger. He slipped on the Mahagick Goggle over his cyclops eye and examined his patient. He could see the splotches of coloured swelling, but the lens was adjusted so he visually penetrate the skin seeing the puss under the epidermis. The green Essential-Monplasma was working to radically evaporating the trapped liquid. He gently rolled an arm over left and right nodding.

Sheranda turned around and returned to the bottom step passing Squadron Leader and Team Leader Pulmonary. The wings bumped against them in passing. The leaders were curious and watched as events unfolded.

"Is there anything I can assist?" Sheranda asked stepping forward.

"Yes. Examine Fire Knight Archer, Oriana," he suggested in a casual tone.

"We're gong to bed now, all of us need to be well rested for tomorrow," Squadron Leader recommended stepping forward.

Kidney spoke with an abrupt tone. "My patient is my first concern, sleep will need to wait."

"Sheranda," Pulmonary called out.

"Sheranda is assisting me," Kidney pointed out as he continued to examine the Knight Commander. "I will foster a Mentor ship," he said with a tone arrogance.

The Street Surgeon leaders listened to their graduate students while watching. The other teammates stood on the steps also watching for twenty-five minutes and then the show concluded.

"Sheranda, time for rest," Kidney encouraged and gestured. They stepped out of the infirmary together as stepping off a stage. Sheranda wrapped a single wing around him as he did not fidget or squirm, it was a friendship embrace.

"Kayla," Pulmonary said.

"What is it?"

"I think we have just witnessed a rock star Street Surgeon."

"And certainly an accomplice," Kayla agreed. "The awesome power of caring," she added.

Kidney and Sheranda approached their teammates and were greeted with approval. They made their way up each step as if rising in the heavens.

"Oh, Pulmonary," Kidney spoke while standing at the midway point, the landing, "don't forget to bring your small stuffed toy. It's on the Fire Knight table."

"Right!"

The Sleeping Manlantean

The alarm clock released a scream, "***Wake up!***" It was purposely designed to shock awake heavily sleepers.

Sherrout was wearing only a trim body suit while sleep-floating within a transparent Sleep Chamber inside the Fire Knight quarters. The pipe cleaner attached to his eyeballs were free of the fishbowl in the sleep-floating container, and the bowl was attached to a hook in the upside position. The eyelids opened seeing Frequent Sea Seven knocking the transparency. It was the vibration of the knocking in the liquid surrounding him which caused the eyelids to sense something. He shook his head, clearing away the sleepiness. Responding to the knocking by sticking out a long blue tongue, next he grabbed the fish bowl and slipped it onto the interlocking collar.

The Fire Knight Commander Story

Kidney and Sheranda were at the bottom step descending the stairs and standing in front of them was Fire Knight Archer, Oriana.

"I am really hungry," she admitted.

"Come with us to the table," Sheranda invited the patient.

"Would you not think it wiser to bring food back to Oriana?" Kidney asked.

"I am obviously feeling better."

"I see the clue standing before me," Kidney replied taking her hand and gently giving a tug leading Oriana back to the infirmary. "We will bring you breakfast, and you removed the IV line," he commented. "Lee-Lee, wire the patient back up," he suggested.

"Sure thing."

"How long must I keep myself plugged in?"

"Four more hours," Sheranda said. "Starting... Now! Time log: 7:12 am."

"We will be gone by nine-thirty clock sharp," Squadron Leader said.

"At 11:13/ 15, I can remove it."

"Good enough," Kidney agreed.

The Street Surgeons gathered around Oriana during breakfast. They sat on chairs while listening to her telling a story.

"Commander-Knight Johnny Vlogger is perhaps one of foremost human authorities on Zerthlings because all through his primary years and teen years he dated Zerthala Objibaawad. Zerthala's father was an Ambassador at-Large. The Zerth Embassy was located purposely in Abraham State in the country Canamerica on earth 34567. It's the only state in Canamerica which would make common sense to insert a Zerth Embassy. Zerthala went to Fire Knight Academy, so that's how they met and became peaches and cream. According to gossip they enjoyed chess, as much as they enjoyed canoeing on the lake surrounding Fire Knight Academy Island. I assume they might stroll along the forest paths holding hands. A terrible thunderstorm loomed over Fire Knight landscape a dozen kids were camping in the woods sleeping, Johnny and Zerthala too. Of course I am much younger than Johnny, one hears stories, and he told me stories, but I learned through the grapevine they became the accidental King and Queen during graduation," Oriana said. "They got engaged just after graduating," she added.

The Street Surgeons exchanged expressions at the end of Oriana's story.

Squadron Leader nodded accepting the story. "While creeping about Lucifer City, Oriana, can you describe the texture, the environment, odors, damp, funky, and people: how are the Zerthlings within the city walls?"

Lee-Lee Southfly laid a reassuring hand on Oriana's shoulder. "If you can give us some physical description before we depart Fire Knight Forte it would be appreciative," he said.

"Is this a single word description?"

"What word would you select?"

"Horrible."

The Street Surgeons all nodded.

"Pulmonary, make contact with Ambu-Lance," Squadron Leader said, "our medical ship will still be at our original touch down zone waiting for us to make contact. We did not make contact when arrived last night. My bad," she admitted.

"If the Epiderpuss Pocket is widely spread --."

Greenie interjected. "Zerthlings' possess a natural immunity --."

"Sterilization," Sherrout spat out.

"Sterilization of a hostile organism preventing it from infecting others, is well within the Street Surgeon ethics," Frequent Sea Seven pointed out.

"The Ambu-Lance does possess the capability of saturating a city even as large as Lucifer and neutralize a hostile organism," Kidney agreed.

"During my time on Teenworld," Squadron Leader began, "after the defeat of Warlord Adolf. He escaped capture. The Moonsteep Medical Empire launched eighteen Ambu-Lances to neutralize all the crap leftover, the atmosphere was thick with fumes, toxic chemicals chewing at the sky and the tens of thousands ill stricken by noxious odors," she said.

Kidney hugged his upper torso with both arms, feeling a depth of emotion, not as deep as the abyss, but deep enough. "The Sterilization Program is well within the Twelve Zodiac Multiverses Medical Law. The Moonsteep Medical Empire performed such a War on Life on planet Gartharian, and that historical moment happened before Teenworld," he pointed out.

Frequent Sea Seven hair unwrapped itself and puffed into a ball of hair.

Sherrout's finger slid around the top portion of the fish bowl and produced three distinct pings instead of snapping his fingers. "I remember that lesson in Medical History Class," he said,

"Gartharian, various optic nerve global supply chains collapsed sending the global economy into a swirling whirlwind tizzy. The food supply chains like dominions wiping out those services in twenty-four hours, followed by the medical supply chains crashed the moment the Gartharian during the same period. The five major global labour unions were sent into a tizzy and tens of millions of low working Gartharians had not job to go to. And then the Pandemic hit with the force of a thunderstorm and lightning speed. The Moonsteep Medical Empire, arrived but and it became to a War to Save Lives, although an official recorded measure sixty-five deaths, the Gartharians argue twenty-three million. We know the truth," Prince Sherrout said.

"Gartharian's economics were put under Perestroika by the celestial being calling Itself, Gorbachev," Frequent Sea Seven remarked.

The Next Step

The Street Surgeons dressed in their body hugging uniforms stood facing Fire Archer-Knight Oriana. The group stood at the exit door ready to leave.

"I will watch over Johnny," Oriana said dressed in a Fire Knight uniform. She could feel her bones were strong as her mind tingled with a confidence. "I will be ready for when you return to pick us up," she assured.

Lee-Lee Southfly and Salvo pulled open the heavy interior door. The Street Surgeons stepped out.

"Close the door and don't open it even if the postman knocks," Pulmonary remarked deadpanning.

"I had no clue the postman stopped by this Fire Knight Fort," Oriana replied scratching her hair confused. "If that was a joke, sorry guys, maybe my mind if cluttered with all the recent action," she admitted.

The Street Surgeons all responded with two thumbs up. And then the interior door closed.

The Secret Warehouse

Standing outside the inner door the Street Surgeons stood within a narrow tunnel of brick and peeling plaster. They could only see this decor using the Mahagick goggles turning night into day.

The Street Surgeon boots slopped through a quarter inch of skin-like water, tiny bones floated. The two inch Mahagick sole gave them an elevator lift. Their feet were well protected from the stew of water.

"The drainage system must be clogged, it will need be cleaned," Lee-Lee Southfly commented.

"This section of the Fire Knight Fort with Lucifer City is a quarter of a mile, built underground," Greenie said, "and it's undetectable from above because it wraps underneath a warehouse. It was built long ago by the Mahagick Engineers. And when we get to the end, we will go up a flight of steps to a secondary door and thus enter the warehouse. The exterior door will blend in with the warehouse wall which has a giant mural of creatures, people and a cool image of Lucifer City. We will go through the warehouse to an exit door located inside a spacious opening surrounded by other buildings. It's a dilapidated zone of Lucifer City, which is owned by several companies established by Fire Knight Associates," she explained.

Frequent Sea Seven picked up on the unspoken and implied words 'Fire Knight Associates'. "In other words Lucifer City recognizes this zone officially owned by foreign powers, off-world, off multiverse and therefore and this zone is considered landscape for a secret embassy."

"I will point out the location of the embassy," Greenie said continuously walking. "And you just smacked down a Zerth fly, metaphorically speaking, assuming this area is owned by a secret embassy. The Lucifer Government will not speak who actually owns the land," she added.

The group ascended a flight of stairs arriving a secondary landing at facing a door. Mounted on the side was a box with symbols not numbers.

"A symbol lock," Kidney said.

"I know the correct symbols." Greenie stepped forward and punching symbols. ***Beep-Beep Da-Da-Da Ting-Tong-Ting Beep-Beep***.

"What if there is a new set of symbols?" Sheranda asked.

"The symbol lock is based on fingerprints."

"Zerthlings don't have fingerprints," Kidney pointed out.

"Not that the fingerprints that can be seen by the naked eye," Greenie replied. "We have fingerprints, I can assure you," she added pressing symbols.

"I had not thought of that possibility," Frequent Sea Seven admitted.

The door swung open squeaking all the way until it stopped.

"This area has roughly fifty warehouses," Greenie continued. "Although I was born in Spirit of Seven Cowboys, things as all of you area aware of, I am very familiar with Lucifer City," she added emerging into a sprawling and empty warehouse.

The warehouse concrete floor was pale, chipped and had splotch marks. A heap of garbage was in the middle area, piled nearly to the roof. It contained a spool of plastic like rope, and planks used for pallets, mixed with paper, debris and shards of glass.

Upper windows along the ceiling, some were broken allowing fowl to take refuge in the rafters. They squawked, screeched, chirped and chattered as though this was an inside jungle.

Moss clumped in patched covering portions of the floor. Slithering creatures lived in the moss.

The open guts of Zerth mice and rats littered the floor.

The door closed and as the Street Surgeons moved forward, the door closed automatically. It locked. Salvo cranked his head around. His eyes gazed upon the wall. He stepped backwards opening his eyes wider. His jaw opened awestruck. Covering the whole wall just as Greenie described was an intricate mural. The mural was seventy feet long and fifty feet high and full of life depicting images. Salvo pressed a button on belt buckle and started snapping up images using the micro-cam built into the Mahagick goggles. He tapped Salvo on the shoulder urging his teammate to turn around. Sheranda paused turning and catching Frequent Sea Seven's attention. The entire Street Surgeon troop gazed for a moment at the mural.

"Holy frogcats!" Kidney said shouting out the name of a Moonsteep creature mostly found in his Swamp Nation.

"The colour has not faded in centuries," Greenie said. "The painter must have used Mahagick paint," she added.

Shrieking

Squadron Leader gestured to Sheranda. The two spread open their wings and whooshed up to get a bird's eye view.

Immediately several Zerth birds rushed in an ambush mode.

Squadron Leader and Sheranda responded shrieking with inhuman vocal abilities, a sweet hidden ability much like the appendage. Such power ripped through the Zerth birds. They quickly flapped their wings mid-flight. They darted away in the opposite thinking a pair of larger creatures were about to eat them!

A portion of the warehouse looked as though it had experienced fire at point as the eastern wall was black, soot from a fire.

The industrial complex of the warehouse consisted of interconnecting pipes, conveyor belts with multi stack rows of mechanical robotic arms stopped in mid-action. The metal hands were clasping onto parts and pieces of something to be assembled, but never got completely finished. Human-like droids stood in various locations and were frozen on the stop. They were silver/ grey in colour and eight feet tall. Some of the droids were headless, over time they may have popped off and dropped next to their metal legs. Or perhaps they were ambushed by a hostile enemy and had their heads clearly slashed off.

Squadron Leader gestured to Sheranda to return to the ground.

“Not a ghost is hunting this warehouse, just creep critters and the ancient world we see around here,” she reported to the troop.

“Should we set our Mahagick pistols on Freeze Mode rather than Stun Mode?” Pulmonary asked.

“F-M mode,” Squadron Leader repeated.

A bloodcurdling screech came without warning.

A Fire Knight in Action

(Kickstart My Heart, Motley Crue)

The Street Surgeons froze. In a moment a heart beat they froze.

Greenie Beanie Jeanie reaching behind back swiftly withdrew the Fire Knight Evergreen Phyre Sword. Pressing the grip the primordial energy sprang up into an incandescent green flame. The decades of training had given her an uncanny agility to prepared at perhaps limitless speed. She jumped between the Street Surgeons and slashed downward striking a blow to Moshskeeduu drooling creature slicing off the head and then landing behind it. She swung around and the blade sliced through the torso. She turned around eyes searching for other such creatures. Nothing, nothing at all. Greenie deactivated the Phyre Energy holding the grip. She was not winded. She looked at her friends and they stared gawking at the shortest person of the whole troop.

“A girl must defend herself from evil creatures that stalk their prey and surely bring violence upon them. I am not a damsel in distress,” Greenie said. “I am a Fire Knight.”

A Street Surgeon Battle Zone

KABOOM!

A powerful fireball appeared. Black smoke plumed creating a fabric of mayhem.

Luciferian pedestrians on the streets below scattered and released screams of panic all of taken by surprise.

“Great Spirits,” Sheranda exclaimed pressing a hand against her chest, catching her breath, “how much explosives did you need, Salvo, Sherrout?” Sheranda asked standing in a hallway.

“Enough so we have a hole in the building,” Salvo replied.

“Well, we really woke up the neighbors. The party will be short. It won’t be long before security forces will be swarming all over this sector,” Pulmonary deadpanned.

“We need to transport the captured Fire Knight Troop out through the hole to an extended ramp when the Ambu-Lance arrives,” Sherrout explained. “We needed to punch a hole in the wall,” he added.

“We got one big hole,” Pulmonary agreed still in a deadpan mode.

"Let's find the Fire Knight Troop," Frequent Sea Seven said.

"I have a map provided by Zerth spies," Greenie replied clutching it in her hand.

The Street Surgeons fanned out with the Mahagick pistols pulled out.

"Greenie, do have the stolen floor plans?" Squadron Leader asked in an urgent tone.

"Right here," Greenie repeated.

A shrilling alarm was activated.

The sprinkler system started raining upon every floor.

"Follow me," Greenie said urgently, "down this hall and turn right. The lab centre should be at the end of the hall," she explained.

Everything seemed to be moving slow motion, as if watching a movie.

Dropping down through ceiling trapdoors, big head creatures with large toothy jaws. The eyes were located on the sides to give a virtually three hundred degree. The eyelids blinked. The pumpkin orange eyes glowed. The all-black muscular bodies glistened with a natural secreted moisture. It was not stinky, but a friendly hypnotic scent, the aroma capable of overwhelming an opponent with love.

Salvo threw his hands outward blocking the others. He simultaneously reached to the back pack withdrawing a bow grip. His other finger pressed a button on the Street Surgeon Belt Buckle activating the front portion body guard and arm guard. The Nanotech worked quickly and flawlessly. Squeezing the bow grip it immediately flashed up body of a bow and a laser string appeared along with a laser arrow. The process finished in less than ten seconds. He aimed the first arrow at one of the savage creatures and launched the laser arrow. It struck the beast right between the eyes. The creature dropped dead.

Everything switched back to a hyperactive mode.

Greenie opened her eyes in surprise.

"You're a trained Fire Knight, and I am a trained Street Surgeon," Salvo replied.

"I thought you had phobias?" Frequent Sea Seven remarked.

"Not when I am on duty," Salvo replied as a punchline.

The blood thirsty creatures gathered in a group. They made a hissing sound. Odor produced was not subduing their opponents. They wore puzzled expressions. These opponents were not playing by the rules.

A Street Surgeon Battle Zone went into hyperactive mode and including one Fire Knight. Sheranda and Squadron Leader released sonic shrieks popping the eardrums of the intended opponents and disturbing the inner sensory portion of the ear.

Kidney released a growl like a wild beast from a swamp, his home province on Moonsteep, Swamp Nation. His fingernails extended nine inches as his adrenal glands pumped up the volume of fight. All people from Swamp Nation could extend their nails during a brawl. His hands quickly covered with thick dark brown fur like of a bear. The inner DNA of his primal ancestors were kicking in at full speed. He reached out slicing one of the creatures across the chest and punching through the rib cage.

Sherrout removed a grip from the backpack. He squeezed the grip and it activated a spear of pure energy. It was measured a ten feet. He fired the energy spear by squeezing the grip and it smacked a creature piercing it through the chest making a gaping hole.

Frequent Sea Seven hair snapped like a whip. It ***snapped*** one of the creatures in the groin area. The creature responded dancing around in pain. And then it was struck through the back by an energy spear. It flopped forward dropping to the floor.

Pulmonary grew larger fists, three times their regular size of a human. He jumped into the thick of action confronting his opponent as though it was match in ultimate knock down fight. He punched with the fierceness of boxer, non-stop and then an upper-cut to the chin and the creature was sent backwards several feet. Pulmonary jumped on top of the chest and the two wrestled on the floor until the creature was pinned. Suddenly an energy spear stabbed the creature through the heart and Pulmonary looked up seeing Sherrout grinning.

Greenie stood watching with a big cheesy grin. She had no reason to involve herself in the excitement, the Street Surgeons were doing just fine. She saw Pulmonary on top of the creature and watched Sherrout jab a spear through the creature's chest. Immediately bound over to Sherrout raising an arm. "Wiener!"

"You mean, winner," Pulmonary corrected wryly.

"Creature comforts," Sheranda remarked.

"Back to work, enough fun in playground," Squadron Leader ordered.

Ambu- Lance

A flock of Zerth birds flew out of a forest adjacent to a beach and exchanging alien chirps and squawks.

Far away from Lucifer City at the landing point on a pristine sandy beach adjacent a lake covered in a thin eerie greenish lingering fog, sat the ready to-go EMS ship officially named by the Moonsteep Medical Empire as an Ambu-Lance. The crew nicknamed it, Ambu, the name after a famous ancient Moonsteep Bird that which Great Spirit rides upon and Lance, it the medical tool used to cure all species. The top portion was thick saucer shaped obviously for the crew. It contained enough space for additional vehicles probes. The bottom was funnel shaped and that's where a door-ramp had been installed.

Tentacles rose up out of the eerie fog and snatched several Zerth birds in flight, breakfast or lunch. The birds would be an excellent snack.

The flock of Zerth birds scrambled in the air, flapping whole body wings adjusting course to elude capture as more tentacles rose up.

Inside the Optic Nerve sat Commander Pilot Wingnut, former Comet Chaser of one hundred years experience. He belonged for four decades to the wildest and award winning Comet Chaser team under the Hammurabi Platoon and the mentorship of Cyrano D Hammurabi, the grandfather of Sheranda. Pilot was friends with her father, Cyrano D. Hammurabi Jr. Pilot applied to the Ambu-Lance Department desiring a change of pace and got instantly accepted along with a hundred others because the Ambu-Lance Department was running short of excellent navigators.

"The Ambu is fit to fly," sixteen year old Pearl sitting in the co-pilot seat and tapping some information on a terminal. She faced three monitors.

"Are the primordial liquid shields primed?" Pilot asked.

"Yes."

"And what do the liquid shield do compared to regular shields?"

"The primordial liquid shields cushion the impact an energy blast, 'we' the occupants don't feel the energy jolt," Pearl Purple Go-Spirit explained in a student tone. "The primordial liquid shield also as sponge absorbing the energy blast, which 'we' can harness and return fire," she added.

"How thick is the liquid shield?"

"No much thicker than one full centimetre."

"Good enough, Pearl Purple Go-Spirit," Pilot said with a wryly attitude, "Let's go rescue some Street Surgeons and patients," he suggested.

"My Father told me he hand picked you to be my mentor as a pilot so when I turn eighteen and when I get an inter-dimensional ship, after I graduate from pilot school, I will be that further ahead and much more relaxed compared to other Newbeflyers," Pearl said.

"General Go-Spirit has weird taste, because I am unsure why he picked me to be your mentor," Pilot wondered, "there are much better mentors or teachers out there to choose from."

The Ambu-Lance lifted silently. Sand swirled wildly as the ship rose on non-toxic thick kettle steam. At one hundred meters it shifted to a new direction toward Lucifer City.

"Estimated arrival is twelve minutes," Pearl reported. "Engaging cloaking cape," she added turning a knob. A small hologram image showed a yellow field surrounding the Ambu-Lance indicating the cloaking cape was active.

The Secret Lab

The Street Surgeons stood inside a large round room with a doughnut hole and it was stacked five floors down. Pale blue fluorescent light was everywhere. Kidney was back to his normal self, along with his teammates.

"Where are the Fire Knights?" Sheranda asked, "there must be three hundred plus bodies," she added.

"What are all these bodies doing inside these stasis containers?" Sherrout asked.

The double-decker stasis containers each had a person inside, one up and one lower. Sheranda noticed the people inside were secure by waist straps, wrist locks while submerged in Primordial Life Liquid, similar to the womb's amniotic fluid. A tube was inserted their nose and mouths. "*Alive, but frozen. Hyper-sleep, all these people are in some hyper-sleep, but more sophisticated than Moonsteep technology*!" she thought. Cables were spooled and held by a clamp. The prongs fit inside a socket in the ceiling. Built on a steel frame attached to a steel pole and locked together resembling an old fashion milkshake maker. Five double-decker stasis containers were attached to the pole.

"By the gods of Aquaskin race," Lee-Lee Southfly whispered as a peculiar sensation crept through his body. He shook his head, trying to be sure what was really happening was indeed real world. He needed to be sure in every fibre of his bones it was not some extreme delusion. Street Surgeon schooling trained his mind to understand between the fable or fantasies and keep calm. Observe the surroundings and the objects in the room are not booby-traps in disguise. Touching cultural the medallion around his neck unconsciously which all Asquaskinner males and girls at the age of twelve, his fingers followed the engraving. Stopping what he was doing, "*Stop fidgeting*!" he scolded himself inwardly thinking. He gave it a kiss. He needed to believe in a higher power, to get exterior resourceful faith. "Not even our Monsoonsea Goddess could imagine such horror," he remarked.

"Greenie, where would Zerth obtain this level of sleep chamber technology?" Frequent Sea Seven asked in an accusing tone.

"Not from my world." Greenie looked at a device she was holding. "I found our Fire Knights. Up one floor," she said.

"Move," Pulmonary ordered. "Up that ladder!"

Dewskinners, Befour Nation Tribe

On the deck above the Street Surgeons found only the Fire Knights, all the stasis containers were open and empty.

Approaching the terminals Sheranda and Squadron Leader recognized symbols on the keyboard.

"Befour Nation letters, our language. We are Dewskinners, one of tribe within the Twelve Multiverse Tribes. All the tribes together create the Befour Nation and many of our people are scattered across the Multiverse on many worlds. Our people long ago were chased off our home world by the race called, Synopaths a.k.a. TV-Heads," Sheranda remarked running her fingers over the keys. She made a scrunch-curious face examining the controls. Befour Nation weekend schooling had taught Sheranda the history of her people, fortunately she was persuaded by her parents to pay attention after childhood adventures which did not include attending classes. "*My Father gave me a single swat on my butt with a paddle to fix my silly brain and to teach me that education is important. It was only that one time in my life my Father ever felt he needed to punish me in a physical manner, but that single swat echoes in my memory,*" she thought. "Obviously someone who invented this required our language to type in whatever commands," she said.

"We need to quickly unlock the stasis containers," Pulmonary said. "I suggest we can open the topside using a standard vibration mine," he continued and from a knapsack with round hockey puck size gizmo. Attaching it to side portion where the locking mechanism was located it stayed magnetically held. He gestured to the Street Surgeon newbies to do the same.

Sherrout, Salvo, Lee-Lee Southfly, Frequent Sea Seven and Sheranda followed his orders. One by one they attached the hockey puck vibration gizmo. Each one was set for thirty seconds.

Meanwhile, Greenie wandered the area using a hand device scanning continuously. The indicators bar flashed blue, nothing interesting whatsoever, but as she moved further through the area the indicator switched to red – danger. She was standing facing a blank wall. Scratching her hair, puzzled. Instincts kicked in and focusing her vision the pupils aqua-green and became more intense scanning the wall and she could see a slice running straight up to the ceiling, it would be invisible to the naked eye.

"Greenie, what is it?" Squadron Leader asked and approached her friend.

"This wall is hollow!" Greenie withdrew the grip of the Evergreen Sword. The double wall-door burst open knocking her back and sliding across the floor. The grip was jarred from her grasp sliding over the edge dropping further down through a large doughnut hole. She saw five eight feet tall metallic droids march out and armed.

Street Surgeon Battle Zone - Part Two

Simultaneously the topside stasis containers popped open. Liquid poured out saturating the floor. It dripped over the edge of the doughnut hole. Upon reacting to the air, the liquid became slime. Kidney slipped and fell against his left arm. He scrambled, struggling back to his feet, and reaching out grabbing the railing pulling himself to his feet.

Sheranda withdrew from the Street Surgeon Utility belt several poker chip size gizmos. Whipping the poker-gizmos toward the five eight feet tall metallic droid they exploded releasing intense blinding light. Flash bombs. The goggles the Street Surgeons wore automatically responded to the brightness and the lens turned super duper black, blocking the flashes.

The Droids sensors upon receiving the impact of bright flashes, it stunned the computer visual system.

Sheranda and Squadron Leader grabbed a hold the Fire Knights. They were plunked upon their shoulders like a fireman carry mode. Their wings whooshed open and they leaped over the railing back down the original level and flew them through a hall to the waiting zone.

Frequent Sea Seven used her hair wrapping around a Fire Knight carefully held the person. Next, she jumped on top of the railing perching there waiting and upon seeing Sheranda returning released the Fire Knight, unwrapping her hair and spilled the Fire Knight into Sheranda's arms.

Salvo and Sherrout once again withdrew their Mahagick Pistols and taking aim at the five eight feet tall metallic droids. They released F-M, the freeze mode. A wall of ice was created. The droids started punching the ice wall.

Kidney withdrew his Mahagick Pistol. He adjusted the knob and shot a Web strand to the floor below and wrapped the other end the railing. He picked up two young Fire Knights, stacked upon one shoulder. He mounted the railing and slipped off holding the Web strand with one hand and sliding to floor below and narrowly dodging energy shots from the droids. He landed safely.

Greenie jumped over the railing and dropped through the doughnut. She withdrew a standard Fire Knight Mahagick Whip and a wrist-flip the end of the whip snagged the railing. It allowed her to fall, fall, fall and fall as she looked for the Evergreen Sword grip and she saw it seven floors doors down. The grip was sitting on the edge. She twisted the whip-grip and manipulated her body swinging over the railing. Attaching the whip-grip to the Fire Knight Utility she simultaneously landed safe, a foot away from the grip. Grabbing the

Evergreen Sword grip she placed it back inside the backpack. Smoothly, she gave the Mahagick Whip a tug and whooshed back up through the hole back up.

Landing behind the five eight feet tall metallic droid, she had not intended this situation, but luck played into the issue. Miracles do happen within the Fire Knight world when fighting for justice. Switching the Mahagick Whip away, she withdrew the Evergreen Sword and the Mahagick Phyre appeared. No time could be better. Slashing at the droids she managed to slice off arms, legs, torsos and heads. The heads rolled over the edge down through the doughnut hole. The dumb-ass droids had no idea what hit them.

"Let's go!" Pulmonary urged shouting gesturing return to the level below and to the escape zone.

Salvo and Sherrout put their Mahagick Pistols away and obeyed the command. They climbed back down the ladder.

Lucifer City

Standing in the room where the giant hole in the building, the pick up zone, the Street Surgeons were caring for the Fire Knights. The utility belt contained all the equipment required to place the patients into the Moonsteep Miracle Comas, sustaining their life.

The Ambu-Lance arrived over Lucifer City. Pilot could see hundreds of skyscrapers, forty, sixty, one hundred and fifty storeys displayed on the monitor. The tallest had landing pads extending out for ships to land and take-off. It stood a staggering five hundred meters and was the designated sky-port. The buildings were crammed together in the centre on the city. The walled city was also cloaked by grubby clogging smog. He swerved avoiding smacking into various flying vehicles, even the cloaking cape was rendering the ship invisible, he knew the aviators would not see the ship.

"I am receiving homing signal," Pearl said listening to the communication. "The Lucifer City Government is unaware the my bloodline, Go-Spirit, is part owner of this ugly city. My ancestors made a business deal with several other Multiverse Business people about forming a secret embassy," she added.

"I think you had better keep your lips tightly sealed, Pearl," Pilot snapped, "secrets are supposed to be secrets. Learn this lesson," he ordered.

"Sssorry."

"Don't be sorry, appreciate you spilled a few beans to my ears," Pilot told her. "I am glad your Father, the General, hand picked me to mentor you," he hinted.

"You won't tell people?" she asked.

"That's the plan, kid," he said wryly as a swashbuckler would deliver a hearty punchline. "Okay, give me the homing signal co-ordinance," he said.

"Steer 3:12 West," Pearl replied.

Pilot punched the co-ordinance into the punch pad informing the computer. The navigation wheel turned automatically and then released control back to him.

The warning alarm sounded, obnoxious loud.

"We have bogeys," Pearl said and switched off the warning system.

"How many?"

"Seven." Pearl whistled.

"No time to whistle me a tune, charge up the defence."

"But, we're protected by the cloak cape."

"The Zerth Internal Air Force could easily possess sophisticated instruments which can detect disturbances or vibrations in the air. Always remember the cloak cape bends light only, it doesn't mean energy waves air molecules cannot be detected. And besides, the Ambu-Lance will need to be visible to pick up the Street Surgeons and guests," Pilot explained looking at the black girl from the multiverse earth-like world numbered 23456.

"The smog of Lucifer City is a stew with too many vegetables," Pearl remarked looking at the monitor.

"Vegetables, try gunk," Pilot teased.

"Pilot, does Zerth possess those type of aircraft?" Pearl asked. "I am punching up the Library Mode to get an inventory list of Zerth air defences," said.

Pilot shook his head. His purposely tapped the Library Mode off. "Never mind. Zerth will not share that information," he said. "Our goal now is to find, rescue and get out of Zerth and back home to Moonsteep," he explained.

Rescue and Battle

"Pilot, we are waiting," Squadron Leader said looking out through the big hole.

Suddenly the Ambu-Lance appeared and a ramp was already extended four inches inside the hole.

"Ready to receive everyone," Pearl replied sitting in the co-pilot seat and seeing the Street Surgeons with the Fire Knights on portable hand carry stretchers. The capes of their uniforms were used as carry stretchers. Everything they wore was purposely designed to harnessed in battle to help in a rescue the wounded.

"Grab the capes and lift!" Pulmonary ordered.

Rushing down the ramp arrived six Clone Nurses, standard crew for an Ambu-Lance. The footwear clanked on the metal mesh. The Clone Nurses were male and female. They helped lift the capes assisting the Street Surgeons up the ramp and inside.

BOOM! BOOM!

"Bogeys on approach!" Pearl sounded off the alert.

"Bogeys are bullies," Pilot replied with swashbuckling attitude. "Angel the defence shield, port side," he ordered.

Pearl obeyed and quickly pressed two buttons.

The Ambu-Lance got thumped again.

BOOM! BOOM!

"Pilot, we're all aboard," Squadron Leader said speaking communicating through the helmet radio. Simultaneously she tapped the side button and the Nanotech shrank the helmet back inside a gizmo pocket at the back of the neck. Running through the circular hall to the Optic Nerve where the pilots sat. "Pilot, we need to pick up two people at the Fire Knight Fort," she continued.

"Fire Knight Fort?" Pilot asked.

"Where is Fire Knight Fort?" Pearl asked.

Greenie arrived at the Optic Nerve. "Fly 7:17," she commanded.

BOOM! BOOM!

"Power on the port shield does not look good," Pearl said. "Down by twenty-seven percent," she remarked.

"Let's go pick up more Fire Knights," Pilot agreed steering the Ambu-Lance away from the building.

KABOOM!

The building was thumped by a powerful torpedo by one of the alien craft. The torpedo struck the building. It exploded into smithereens!

The ramp snapped back into a rest place. Next, an aperture slid into place tucking the ramp safe. The exterior wall-door slid down and locked secured. The whole process took less than thirty seconds.

Sheranda and Kidney were somehow left behind. Things were happening too fast. When the building began crumbling they leaped out of the hole.

"There gone!" Sherrout exclaimed in horror.

Wings and a Prayer

Kidney continued falling through thick dust and debris. His legs and arms were kicking. "*The Street Surgeon parachute. Pull it! Pull it*!" he told himself, but the surrounding debris was distracting him. He narrowly collided into a chunk of metal. He felt something strong grab him and first he reacted resisting, but he saw a person, the face of an angel.

Sheranda's wings whooshed open like a parachute. Changing her body position with smoothness, she dove and flapped the wings. It took less than a minute for her to catch up to Kidney and she snatched him from the death fall. Next, she changed her body position and flapped hard several times returning to the sky. Some how she saw a large Zerth Screecher-Byrd, a beak capable of crushing a victim with one crunch. She dropped down on top of the Ambu-Lance. Upon releasing Kidney they ducked low avoiding the Screecher-Byrd.

Right Back to Business

"This way to the hatch, Sheranda!" Kidney pointed in the direction and she nodded. "I*gnore what just happened, this type situation does happen and will happen as a Street Surgeon. I am appreciative Great Spirit gave me Sheranda Hammurabi as a guardian angel*," he thought. Holding hands they ran across the top of the saucer to the hatch.

Salvo stood in the Gathering Area of the Ambu-Lance. He heard a noise from above and curiously watched the hatch open. Friends descended.

"We're hitching a taxi ride home to Moonsteep," Kidney quipped.

"Out dating," Salvo accused countering with his own wit, "we have patients aboard," he scolded in a serious playful manner.

"I did not enjoy the fall, but trip wasn't so terrible," Kidney replied padding himself. "My internal parachute would not deploy," he continued with a slightly different tone.

"Say hello to my cheesy date," Sheranda played up the fun with a one-liner. Why not continue the fun?

Suddenly the parachute deployed. It covered Salvo.

Sherrout walked into the Gathering Area as if on cue and got captured by the chute.

"Cut the straps," Salvo and Sherrout insisted annoyed.

Lee-Lee Southfly walked into the Gathering Area and sizing up the situation in less than ten seconds, performed an about-face and left.

Bianca Blaze Teenage Fire Knight

Regrouping in Infirmary, Sheranda and Kidney worked with the Clone Nurses examining a patient sitting upright on the medical bed.

"Why are you not lying down?" Sheranda asked.

"My name is Bianca Blaze, and he is my boyfriend, Ford Horseman," she said trying to shake off the shivers. She brushed out of her face long, dirty blonde stringy hair. "*There is not place on Zerth for a real shower, and at this moment, I don't give a shit. I want to go home,*" she thought. "We are from earth 34567. Ford and Myself were conducting an investigation, clues showed us that one of the Fire Knights was not one of us, not human, not born on earth 34567. He is a Zerthling, but also traitor. We were both abducted by Master Fire Knight Brumblebeetle and placed inside an inter-dimensional cylindrical rocket ship and sent to planet Zerth. We have survived on Zerth for two and half years. We used every trick in the Fire Knight survivalist book to keep alive, before meeting up by accident with Fire Knight Troop, Mercer Ryder," she explained while wrapping her around herself trying to stop shivering. "I am now twenty-one," she added and began crying.

"Your face is slight naturally coloured blue, therefore I assume you are a member of Befour Nation Tribe," Sheranda accused with a gentle assertive tone.

"The Blue People Tribe," Bianca admitted wiping away tears.

"Well, Bianca, welcome aboard the Moonsteep Ambu-Lance," Kidney said in a quiet tone, "but we insist you lay down and let us do our job," he added gesturing to medical bed.

"The Moonsteep Embassy and when the Fire Knights wake up, we will get you and your boyfriend home," Sheranda assured.

Next Up!

"Sheranda, come with me," Squadron Leader ordered stepping inside the Infirmary. "Together we will help bring Oriana and Johnny Vlogger aboard," she explained.

"Do want assistance?" Salvo asked.

"No. This should not take long," Squadron Leader replied. "We can fly in and back faster than walking," she added.

Pulmonary approached and both a brand new powered up pair of Street Surgeon Utility Belts. They removed the first handing them over to one of the Clone Nurses.

"I will restock the utility belts," the Clone Nurse said and took them away.

And two new Mahagick Pistols were slid inside holsters.

Sheranda followed Squadron Leader through the central hall to the turbo lift.

"Five minutes," Pearl spoke over the PA, "five minutes is all we give. You will be luck to get two and half," she added.

"Over and out," Squadron Leader replied.

The turbo lift door closed.

The turbo lift door opened and in stepped Greenie holding a Mahagick Pistol. "I am accompanying both of your as your official bodyguard," she said.

Sheranda exchanged a surprise expression with Squadron Leader. The Dewskinner woman stood a good two and a half feet taller than Greenie, perhaps the image of the short person on a basketball team, very dangerous.

"Short-stop," Sheranda teased.

"Who put you in charge?" Squadron Leader asked acting a teenage girl who just bumped as the captain of a cheerleader squad.

"Insults and bad jokes will not deter me from performing my duty as your bodyguard," Greenie said in a causal tone. She sighed. She grinned. "Remember, Johnny Vlogger was infected with Epiderpuss-pocket and it's an air-born. "Activate your helmets," she ordered.

The Street Battle

(Kickstart My Heart, Motley Crue)

The turbo lift door opened.

Greenie zoomed out first. Sighting Zerthlings she immediately began squeezing the Mahagick Pistol trigger. The laser guided targeting system allowed each Nano-size dart to strike a person without remorse, without being intercepted. It was not whether or not people were and/ or infected, everyone was going to get a shot. She resembled a wild-west shooter. "*These people are my brothers and sisters, we are Zerthlings. Our home world, Zerth has become a foster child within the Twelve Zodiac Multiverses, a world once all other worlds envied. These people need a booster shot to ward off Epiderpuss-pocket, a common virus on Zerth. I am going to deliver the home remedy with the determination of a Fire Knight*," she thought. Each person smacked with the Nano-size dropped on the spot and began shaking and gradually convulsion. The booster serum worked extremely quickly. They would stop convulsion with fifteen minutes. They would come around with a hangout affect. It would take a full day to recuperate Examining the counter, it now indicated zero. Greenie had emptied two thousand Nano-size darts in less than sixty seconds. The sidewalk was covered in bodies.

Greenie discharged the wafer magazine by pressing a button. Withdrawing from the Fire Knight utility belt a new wafer thing magazine she slipped inside the slot and it locked automatically. Next, the vial on the top of the Mahagick Gun she snapped it off and tossed it. From the utility belt she withdrew a new vial and connected it and the liquid quickly filled the inner tank. The indicator showed green.

Classified as a Superhero

Half a dozen alien ships began swarming over Lucifer City.

Sheranda and Squadron Leader performed a leap-fly and touched down landing at the warehouse. The door slid open. They took three steps back taken by surprise. Oriana was holding a groggy and dazed Johnny Vlogger.

"Smack on time," Sheranda said.

"Hold on, we're flying you back to the Ambu-Lance," Squadron Leader remarked.

Energy bolts rained upon the zone of warehouses. Plumes of debris appeared.

"This will cause some inter-dimensional crisis," Green said.

"Fly!" Squadron Leader ordered taking hold of Oriana, securing underneath the armpits. Lifting up smoothly it was a mere leap-fly, nine meters to the turbo lift.

Greenie dashed back to the turbo lift moving at bionic speed, legs propelling her at a solid one hundred and sixty kilometres per hour. "*This is less than a quarter of my true velocity, during Fire Knight training I learned in my DNA I am classified as a Superhero. I topped the speed of the sound barrier*," she thought. Standing inside the turbo lift along with her teammates and guests, she continuously pressed the door close symbol. And after a few times the door closed.

"Pilot, get us all out of Lucifer City," Squadron Leader ordered. "Get everyone home, back to Moonsteep!"

The Hey-Zeus Suspension Bridge

(Kickstart My Heart, Motley Crue)

Pearl Purple Go-Spirit punched into the punch-pad information.

"Tell me what you're doing?" Pilot asked demanding.

"The Ambu-Lance is set for Moonsteep, step on the pedal!" she instructed.

Pilot shifted the gearshift and stepped hard on the pedal.

Displayed on the monitor appeared ringlets of coloured lights stretching into infinity. The ship slipped inside a supernatural tunnel of primordial liquid energy spinning counterclockwise. It was a tunnel of neither not classified as a 'Wormhole' or a 'Black Hole', but it the Mahagick People classified as a 'Suspension Bridge' and the Faithful had always called it, 'The Hey-Zeus Bridge'. It was the Primordial Bridge to All-Multiverses. Travelling on the Primordial Frequency, Zilohertz would be of one method of a supernatural resource, but there were two others.

"At current Zilohertz Frequency the Ambu-Lance will arrive back at Moonsteep from Zerth in eighteen minutes," Pearl said aware of the time factor. "If the Ambu-Lance could move at Virilian Frequency our time Factor would be nine minute," she added.

"Any of those ships following us?" Team Leader Pulmonary asked entering the Optic Nerve.

"Nothing on my sensors," Pilot replied confident.

"Mission accomplished," Pearl said exchanging the classic fist-touch with Pilot.

Moon steep/ Pangaea

Akhenaten City, a city of circular buildings, doughnuts, some with a hole and some filled in. A portion of the Akhenaten landscape was a desert purposely left uninhibited as it was specifically used for inter-dimensional travel purposes, in-coming and departures to the Twelve Zodiac Multiverses. Ships arriving entered out of thin-air as the expression goes and quickly lower to the runway with yellow lights and soon touch down in the red zone adjacent the Global Airport. The ships in the departure mode would taxi off the green zone.

Ear-splitting thunder sounded. The sky ripped like tearing a piece of paper. Ringlets of endless appeared briefly as the Ambu-Lance was spat out Exotic Space and into the Moonsteep world.

Pilot reached up above his head and twisted a knob. The Ambu-Lance sirens kicked as all EMS vehicles would announce themselves. The siren and the distinct symbols on the sides of the ship made every ship aware and traffic slowed. Two cruisers slid along side with flashing red and white lights giving a courteous escort not to the red zone but the Moonsteep Medical Tower with several landing pads extended out fingers.

"Confirmed," Pearl said listening to Traffic Control through her earpiece. "Pilot, docking station three," she reported.

The Ambu-Lance arrived, hovered and lowered a steam on docking station three two minutes later.

A flurry of medical personnel accompanied by Clone Nurses rushed out of the building over to the Ambu-Lance pushing float gurneys. They met the Street Surgeons pushing the Fire Knights out of the turbo lift.

Ten minutes later the Fire Knights were wisked inside the hospital.

What to do next

Two days later.

The Street Surgeon, Kidney, Sheranda, Salvo, Sherrout, Lee-Lee Southfly, Frequent Sea Seven were sitting around a table in a room. The walls were navy blue. Sunshine was dimmed by a thin blind.

"Greenie is not one of us, a Street Surgeon," Team Leader Pulmonary said sitting next to Squadron Leader Kayla, "she will be returning to earth 34567 when the Fire Knight Troop is ready. Her mission was to help us rescue the Fire Knights." He gave nod to Kayla.

"Your reports and self evaluation of your performances will be expected within the week," Kayla said as her wings quivered in a natural way. "This was your first live action field operation, and with what I witnessed each of you, good stuff. All of you will be on a twenty-five year probationary period as part of your graduation into the Street Surgeon life. And after twenty-five years you will be allowed to select assignments according to situations. Our Moonsteep DNA allows us to live with a Superhero Lifespan as all of you aware," she explained opening a small box removing ID Badges and like a Black Jack player, flicked each one to one of the Street Surgeons.

Sheranda's wings stretched and relaxed. One of the wings bumped against Kidney and he exchanged a wryly expression. Switching her attention to the ID Badge is had a holographic picture and below: **STREET SURGEON 1221/ SHERANDA QARLETTE HAMMURABI.... Moonsteep Medical Empire 0097654312&.**

"Street Surgeons, welcome to a brand new life and a brave new face," Pulmonary said and stood up. "We will call you back in a month. Dismissed!"

The Street Surgeons could not resist the building temptation. They embraced each other in celebration. A wash of emotion came over each member. The mission had brought them together as a family of care givers of an uncanny nature on an alien world, Zerth.

"Sheranda, would you like to take train trip with me to Swamp Nation?" Kidney asked.

"Are you asking me out on a date?"

"An adventure," he replied.

"What type of adventure?" Sherrout asked.

"A Moonsteep adventure, I guess."

"Count me in," Frequent Sea Seven agreed.

"Me too, and Salvo," Lee-Lee Southfly said.

"My phobias need exercising and Swamp Nation sounds like a good spot," Salvo replied.

Kidney looked at all his friends. "I ask one person and everyone want to tag along. I am impressed," he remarked and suddenly Sheranda hooked his arm in friendship and together walked out of the office.